CW01659044

THE TOFF ON FIRE

"I'll tell you what," said Rollison, "I'll make a deal. If you come into this room bringing the baby with you, Maggie, I'll just take you and the baby, and beat it. I won't tell the police where I found the precious infant, I'll just let it be a warning to the Doc. He'll be intrigued to find out whether I can make Maggie talk, too. Yes?"

Leo had moved a few inches from the wall. He was going to spring forward, fling himself into the big room, and shoot Rollison. His lips were parted, and his teeth showed; he had an ugly, savage look.

"No, I perceive," went on Rollison, as if sorrowfully. "I was afraid not. I'd better ring the police——"

Then, Leo spoke.

"If you call the police, I'll cut the kid's throat," he said, and sounded as if he meant it.

Maggie stood stock still, looking down at the child, listening to that unending *brrr-brrr-brrr*. After Leo's threat there was no sound and no movement from the other room; it was almost as if Rollison had vanished into thin air.

Also by the same author,
and available in Coronet Books:

A Bundle for the Toff
The Toff at the Fair
A Six for the Toff
The Toff and the Fallen Angels
Model for the Toff
Double for the Toff
Vote for the Toff
The Toff and the Trip-Trip-Triplets
The Toff and the Runaway Bride

The Toff on Fire

John Creasey

CORONET BOOKS
Hodder Paperbacks Ltd., London

First published by
Hodder and Stoughton Ltd., 1957
Coronet edition 1967
Second impression 1974

Made and printed in Great Britain for Coronet Books, Hodder Paperbacks Ltd., St. Paul's House, Warwick Lane, London, EC4P 4AH, by Cox & Wyman Ltd., London, Reading and Fakenham

ISBN 0 340 02415 1

CONTENTS

1

THE DARK STREET

It was very dark.

The street lamps, high and distant, shed only a little light, and left most of the doorways of the tall, narrow houses in deep shadow. These were terraced houses in London's Mayfair, each as close to its neighbour as Siamese twins, each as remote from its neighbour as a man from his past. Not far off there were sounds of traffic, none loud, none which disturbed the quiet here. Occasionally a car or taxi, sidelights glowing, passed the end of the street, but no vehicle and no person had turned into the street for twenty minutes.

There were some lighted windows, fanlights which showed a black number in silhouette, and here and there amid the gloom a house was painted white or cream, looking as if it was giving off a faint, ectoplasmic glow.

A clock struck, nearby, a booming *one*! A listener might have waited with growing impatience and some tension for the stroke of two, but it did not come. It was one o'clock in a gloomy street on a dark, moonless night. A different sound drew near, sharper and closer, the unmistakable sound of a motor-cycle with a two-stroke engine. A pale, yellowish glow appeared at one end of the street—the one which led to Piccadilly some hundred yards away. It came on quickly, the beam lengthening as the motor-cycle roared. The driver's foot scraped along the road, and in his ears there was a sharp hissing sound. The woman riding behind him, astride the pillion of the machine, drew in her breath. The driver made no comment, but switched off the engine and coasted towards the kerb. Now the only sounds were those of the tyres on the smooth road, and the man's right foot scraping as he made sure that he did not fall.

He stopped, with one foot on the kerb to steady himself and the machine. He turned his head, but was not looking at the woman or the bundle she carried; he was staring towards the street from which he had just come. The woman, little more than a girl if the faint light from the nearest street lamp was a true indication, stared tensely at him. Her eyes and his were shiny and bright, as with fear.

The bundle lay unmoving in the woman's arms. She glanced down at the grey shawl which covered the infant, leaving just a gap at the face.

There were great tears in the woman's eyes.

Suddenly, the man said: "Okay, we've dodged 'em. You get off."

"Are—are you sure?" She had a low-pitched, unsteady voice.

"If you hang around much longer they'll find us again," the man said roughly, and he twisted round and put out a hand to steady her. She climbed off awkwardly, holding the child very tightly. As soon as she was standing on the pavement, the driver sprang off the machine and began to push it towards the middle of the houses on the right-hand side. The machine made little noise, nor did the man's footsteps, but the woman's heels tapped sharply, and the man kept glancing down at them. Suddenly, he rasped in a hoarse whisper:

"Why don't you walk on your toes?"

The woman caught her breath again, hissingly, but obeyed. Carrying the child while raised on her toes all the time, she looked as if she might pitch forward. She couldn't stay on tiptoe, but when down on her heels again she walked less heavily, and the man did not protest again.

He kept looking over his shoulder, but no one else turned into the street, and the noises were all from Piccadilly, or from further afield.

"How—how much further is it?" the woman dared to ask.

"Nearly there."

"Dan, you're sure——"

"You wanted to bring him as much as me." The man spoke impatiently and almost too loudly, and as soon as he stopped he peered over his shoulder again; this time he missed a step. He banged his shin against a pedal of the motor-cycle, swore, and stared fearfully towards the car which appeared at the end of the street.

It went past.

They came upon a lighted doorway, and the fanlight, in the shape of a large half-moon, bore the number 22, in jet black against frosted glass.

"Okay," the man said.

He stood the motor-cycle up against the kerb, and then took the woman's arm. She was staring at the number on the fanlight, and stood quite still, even when he began to push her. He pushed harder, and she began to move, her gaze switching from the number to the baby. The light here was good enough to show its mouth, its nose, one of its closed eyes. She clutched it tightly as the man hustled her up to the doorway.

"Don't get too near me," the man said. "I want room to move."

He slid something from his pocket, then shone a light on to the lock; a Yale. The woman watched him as if the sight of his dexterity could make her forget her anguish and her fear. The man's long fingers moved with nimble speed, he pushed something into the lock, an instrument which looked as if it was going straight through to the other side. He made little sound, and did not look away from the lock.

Suddenly he grunted; then:

"Okay," he said, and there was a sharp click as the door opened a fraction. He pushed it wider. As he did so, and as the woman moved to go inside, a car engine sounded, the driver changing gear; the car was coming into the street. The man thrust the door wide, pushed the woman inside and jumped after her, closing the door behind him without a sound, then leaned against it, gasping for breath.

This car passed within two yards of the front door.

"Come on," the man said, urgently. "We've got to hurry."

Ahead of them was a wide passage, a closed doorway, and a flight of stairs—stone stairs covered with a haircord carpet of pale red. The stairs had a half landing, and had the woman glanced up she would have seen them spiralling round and round above their heads to the third and top floor. Instead, she stared down at the baby, and she didn't move.

"*Get a move on!*" the man rasped.

She began to breathe very heavily and quickly, as if fighting for breath.

"Dan, I can't do it! I can't leave him, I tell you I can't leave him! I'll have to take a chance, I——"

Instead of pushing her towards the stairs, the man stood quite still. He was small and lean, with very bright, pale grey eyes and heavy, gingery tiny eyebrows. His face was lined and leathery, his eyes puckered with crowsfeet. He moved round so that he could look at her, and took her elbows, so that they stood close with the sleeping child between them.

"Listen, Evie," he said, "he's my kid as well as yours, ain't he?" He paused, clenching his teeth. "If the Doc gets his hands on him, what do you think he'll do? *He* won't give him his ten o'clock feed and put him to bed. God knows what he'd do, but he'd find some way to make me talk. Why don't you realize that, Evie? We've got to get the kid somewhere safe until the heat's off, and the Doc——"

"You'll *never* be free from the Doc!" the woman cried.

She was a woman and this was her child; and she was a girl, certainly not yet twenty, with the lovely, pure skin of youth. She was no beauty, but very wholesome, with a good enough figure and bright, shining blue eyes.

"Everyone will be free from the Doc one of these days," the man growled, "sooner than you expect, p'raps. If I sell to him, I won't get a tenth of what the stuff's worth. But we can't stand here arguing, we've to take the kid upstairs, and then——"

"Dan, I'm sorry, but I *can't* leave him. I can't just put him down outside a door and leave him. I tell you I can't!"

They stood glaring at each other.

In spite of their tension, they spoke in whispers, and their voices did not travel. There was no other sound and no other movement in the house. The closed door opposite the foot of the stairs carried the letter A, and a name on a tiny brass plate: *G. A. Roberts.*

The man gripped the girl's elbows so tightly that it must have hurt.

"Listen, Evie, be yourself! Rollison will look after the kid, he won't let it come to any harm——"

"How do you *know*?" she cried. All the torment of her mind quivered in that question. "How can you possibly be sure, how do you know he won't report it to the police, or the newspapers, so that the Doc will know where——"

"Because he wouldn't be Rollison if he did," the man said raspingly. "I know the Toff, don't I? If it was anyone else I wouldn't be so sure, but I know how his mind works, I *know* he won't blab to the rozzers or the ruddy newspapers. He——"

"But——"

"*I tell you I know*," the man said fiercely. "If you won't do it then gimme the kid, and——"

Something in his expression broke the mother's resistance. She closed her eyes, momentarily, then freed herself and began to walk up the stairs. The man followed, and when they reached the first landing, he muttered:

"Two more flights."

The woman was walking on tiptoe now, but that was fairly easy while going upstairs, and she made little noise.

The man made none at all. At the next landing, he pushed past her and went ahead, no longer worried in case she changed her mind; and she followed, her speed slackening only because she was now beginning to breathe heavily.

The man reached the top flat first.

The doorway was painted black, the letter G was painted on it and, black on white at the side of the door, the name: *Richard Rollison.* There was a silver-plated knocker and a silver-plated bellpush and letter box. The man ignored all these, and studied the keyhole, going down on one knee to do so. By the time the mother reached the top of the stairs, the father was already working on this door as he had on the one downstairs; he did his work as easily and naturally as his wife would feed the child.

The door opened, silently, on to darkness.

"Dan, supposing——" she whispered.

"Shut up," the man said. His hissing voice sounded very loud, and betrayed his quivering nerves. "Here, lemme put the kid——"

"I'll do it!"

"For Pete's sake get a move on!"

The landing light shone into the hall, but showed little, except a wine-red carpet, a small picture, and a writing desk of beautifully figured walnut. Two doors stood open. The girl hurried into the hall, holding the child less tightly, and looked about. A large settee, standing slantwise across a corner of this entrance hall, was the obvious place for the child. She crossed to it, while the man went to the writing desk and took a piece of paper and a pencil out of his pocket.

The light here showed that his finger tips were covered with adhesive tape.

He wrote in block capitals, forming each letter clumsily but with great care, and when he finished he looked up with nervous impatience towards his wife.

"Why the hell aren't you ready?" he began.

But for the second time she silenced him without a word. She stood by the side of the couch, looking down upon her child, and on her face there was such despair, in her eyes such tragedy, that the man could neither speak nor move.

There was no sound at all.

Suddenly, the mother swung round on her heels and walked as if blindly towards the door. She did not look at the man. She did not look back at her child. She went out of the flat, across the landing, and started down the stairs, her heels going *tap-tap-tap-tap* as if she had forgotten all need for caution. The man moved after her, closed the door, heard it click, and then hurried so that he could catch up. He did, but she took no notice. Clumsily, he took her arm, but she did not appear to notice that, either. At the last flight he seemed to tire of holding her, and went ahead, opening the front door and peering into the dark street.

Nothing had changed.

He closed the door after the girl had stepped past him, and at last he spoke.

"The kid'll be okay; you don't have to worry. If you knew the Toff as well as I do——"

"Listen, Dan," she said in a taut voice, "I don't want to talk about it. Let's get a move on."

"I'm only telling you."

She didn't speak, but straddled the pillion. The man took his seat, pushed the self-starter with his foot, heard the engine pick up and then fade, started it again and kept it roaring. He moved off, swaying across the road at first, then going steadily until they reached the corner. A car passed the end of the street and he had to wait, but only for a moment. He drove along the narrow streets towards Park Lane, and as he turned a corner saw a policeman standing and looking at him, as if wondering what a motor cyclist and a passenger were doing abroad as late as this.

The little engine went pop-pop-pop-pop, and then the sound faded and the motor-cycle disappeared round a wide corner, leaving the road empty.

Now, the girl sat closer to her man, and after a while she put her arms round his waist, so as to hold on more firmly. He was travelling very fast, as if still fearful of being followed.

He kept looking round, but saw nothing to add to his fears.

2

A GIFT FOR RICHARD ROLLISON

"OH, we can't go home yet," said Esmeralda Gale in a tone of dismay, "it's far too early. Where shall we go?"

Jane Wylie, who was just on the wrong side of forty and showing signs of wanting to slow down, glanced at her watch and said, almost *sotto voce* and longingly:

"It's a little after two."

"That's what I mean," said Esmeralda. Her glittering bracelet was a token, only lately received, of her twenty-first birthday. She looked with rounded green-gold eyes at her aunt. "We just *can't* go home yet, darling. Rolly, don't you know where we could go for a little bit of life? How *dull* London can be! Sometimes I wish——"

"Don't say it," advised Richard Rollison, regarding Esmeralda's round, fresh, pretty face with interest and amusement, "the night life of Gay Paris is not for the likes of you."

"Oh, don't be ridiculous! I was there for three weeks last year, and nothing happened to me!"

"You can't always rely on guardian angels. Do you really want excitement?"

"Oh, *yes*. Rolly, darling, where will you take us? Is it really exciting? Criminal, I mean. It couldn't be Chinatown, could it? Someone once told me——"

"It isn't criminal and it isn't Chinatown; Chinatown is

far too respectable these days. And we are not going to another hot spot at this hour of the morning; they're all flat, half-empty and smelling unpleasantly of stale tobacco. Those idiots who stay after two o'clock are drunk and maudlin or just drunk. No. I thought you might like a drive through London, on a dark night it's quite a thing to do and remember. We might even look in at Scotland Yard, if the chap I know is on duty there——"

Esmeralda's face fell.

"I say, that's not a bad idea," said Sir John Wylie, his eyes lighting up for the first time since they had reached the Star Club, which they had just left because it was too dull to be true. "Prowl cars, Flying Squad, all that kind of thing. How about it, Jane?"

"I'll go with the majority," said his wife, and looked her silent thanks at Rollison for rejecting another night-club, with its giddy noise and its false gaiety, its heat and its haze of tobacco smoke. "Is it likely to be very exciting at Scotland Yard at night?"

"Nothing guaranteed," said Rollison, and waited for Esmeralda to say whatever she had to say now.

They were in a narrow Mayfair Street outside the Star Club. Above their heads was a small star, shaped out of yellow neon, which gave them all a peculiar look of jaundice, and flattered no one, not even the pretty girl. Except for the star and the street lamps, it was very dark. Had he had his way, Rollison would have driven alone round the empty streets, to relish the feel and the smell and the ghost of London at night. For this was his home, and he had a great affection for it.

Recently he had been in the United States for several months, following his peculiar kind of business, and now that he was back, London exerted its unseen influence again.

He knew that he intrigued both Esmeralda and her aunt, but had a suspicion that earlier in the evening Jane Wylie had slightly disapproved. That was not surprising, for he had a reputation for being both a ladies' man and a lady-killer, and of leading a strange life, half in his own milieu of Mayfair, half in London's murky East End.

And this was partly true.

Esmeralda would not disapprove, however wild the rumours. She had already made that obvious, by her eagerness to dance and touch and whisper in his ear while dancing. It was to his eternal credit that he did not take advantage of the many girls of Esmeralda's age and comeliness who found that his good looks, his dark hair with its tendency to wave, and the glints in his grey eyes, were all irresistible. There was an unending string of could-have-been conquests—a host of sweet young things who lived to bless his name.

But Esmeralda——

A gust of wind cut along the street; they would not want to wait much longer. In the distance, thunder rumbled, and the street lights glistened on wet roads and wet pavements. Inside the Star Club, the thunder had sounded even above the band and the dancing, but here and there stars showed, now, and the storm was nearly over.

They waited upon Esmeralda.

That was not only because she was spoiled, but because this was one of a few days' holiday; she wanted to make the most of them, and they were anxious to help her. Waiting, they gazed upon her, and Rollison, who was old enough to think of Esmeralda as being very, very young, saw the light come slowly into her eyes. This was the dawning of some great idea. Rollison groaned, inwardly, for there were far better ways of spending the witching hours than listening to slow music or frenzied bop, drinking indifferent champagne and eating stale sausages.

"*I* know," declared Esmeralda, and took hold of Rollison's hands. "We'll go to *your* flat, and have another drink. You can tell us all about *every*thing."

"It's hard to believe," said Rollison, with some relief, "but there are things about everything which I don't yet know. Come by all means, but are you sure——"

"Of course I'm sure!" cried Esmeralda. "It was talking

about Scotland Yard that made me think of it. Do you know, it's very hard to realize that you are a modern Sherlock Holmes, a kind of——"

"That's almost sacrilege," Rollison reproved. "Don't let anyone with a passion for Holmesiana hear you say it."

"Of course you'd make light of it," scoffed Esmeralda, and she appealed to her aunt for support. "Jane, isn't he a detective? I mean, isn't he a *famous* detective? I mean——"

"Had the shock of my life, once," put in Wylie, as if he meant it. "Had to go and see a chap at the Home Office, happened to coincide with a wave of smash-and-grabbing. You know." Wylie was large and solid, stolid and, by reputation, unimaginative. "Actually heard a VIP from Scotland Yard say to my opposite number, 'what we're going to do is see if Rollison has any ideas'. You might," added Wylie earnestly, "have knocked me over with a piece of straw. Always thought this reputation of yours was newspaper nonsense, Rollison. Isn't, though. Congratulations. Is it true you have a kind of Black Museum at your flat?"

"Black *Museum*?" Esmeralda echoed, almost shrill. "You mean—you mean relics of *crimes* and things?"

"Especially things," agreed Rollison mildly. "The odd knife or two, here and there a gun, a little poison and odds and ends of weapons of assault. You wouldn't be interested at all."

"You brute!" cried Esmeralda, "why didn't you suggest this before?"

She led the way to her uncle's large grey car, and waited for Rollison to get in first. She slid in next to him, leaving the front for Jane and John Wylie. There was just time for Rollison to see Jane's expression, and to realize that she was grateful that they weren't club-crawling; then the doors were closed and Wylie started off, handling the Rolls-Bentley as if it was part of himself.

Those who knew him slightly believed that he was at best an ass and at worst an oaf. He held a high and somewhat vague position in the Foreign Office, he was reputed to be absurdly rich, and until that evening Rollison, judging only from his reputation, would have given him no marks for tact. Yet his mention of a Black Museum had been the deciding factor; and obviously his wife was not the kind of woman who would gladly suffer a fool.

They had met early that evening at a cocktail party, and Wylie had suggested dinner when Rollison had nothing in particular to do. He had been intrigued by Wylie's restrained heartiness, and attracted by his niece, and so he had joined the party. Now he believed that he would always have a healthy respect for Wylie, but their acquaintance was not likely to blossom into a beautiful friendship.

And Esmeralda was too young——

Esmeralda, suddenly, was cuddling close against Rollison, and asking to be kissed. Silently. They passed street lamps and Rollison saw her fair face and her curly golden hair, now in a bright light and now in shadows; there were worse things in life than this. She wriggled so that Rollison put his arm round her shoulders, but he was as impersonal as it was possible to be, and soon she realized it.

He was sorry that it had turned out this way. Esmeralda in a huff at the flat would not be amusing; he would probably regret——

They passed another lamp and he looked down at her, and saw that she was smiling, almost laughing at him. He chuckled gave her a squeeze which made her breathless and then kissed her on the lips. Esmeralda gave a mock sigh, and snuggled comfortably close.

"Gresham Terrace, didn't you say?" Wylie said, without looking round.

"Yes, that's right. Number 22."

"Not far now," said Wylie, and stifled a yawn. "Don't be surprised if I drop off to sleep, will you. Had a heavy day."

"Ha-ha," said Esmeralda, derisively.

"Young people," complained Wylie, "no respect." He turned two corners, and they were in Gresham Terrace, where Rollison had lived for many, many years. The light was still on in the hall, the 22 jet black against the frosted glass. Wylie brought the car quietly to a standstill, and a minute later Rollison was opening the ground floor door. Nothing suggested that it had been forced. He ushered the others in, and although they were not unruly, their footsteps made plenty of noise. By the time they reached the top, Wylie was out of breath.

"Must say this," he said, pausing between words. "My medal goes to the man who invented lifts."

It was dry but it wasn't even slightly funny. Rollison speculated how long the visit would last. Half an hour was too sanguine. An hour? If he judged Jane Wylie aright she would leave for home and bed as quickly as she could. It was now nearly half-past two, so with any luck he would be in bed by half-past three.

He talked, easily, his task to amuse them.

"I'm on my own for a few days, as my man's on holiday; he prefers the autumn to summer. Grieve for me as head cook-and-bottle washer, please." He crossed the hall, and the others followed, the women glancing about them but noticing only that the cushions on the couch were not properly in position. Rollison opened the door of his living-room-cum-study, and went blithely forward, knowing almost to the letter what the others would say and how they would exclaim when they saw what there was to see. First there would be a moment of startled silence; then squeaks; then a grunt or two. And finally Esmeralda would advance across the large room, her eyes glistening, and would touch the hempen rope which hung from a miniature scaffold on his trophy wall, and say:

"Is this a real one? Did it hang a man?"

He would say 'yes', and all three of them would enjoy a few seconds of chills and horror, while he opened the cocktail cabinet and took out the drinks. Esmeralda would then start asking questions. What was the top hat doing at the top of all the exhibits on the wall? Why—oh, was that a *bullet* hole through it? Had he been wearing it when the shot had been fired? *Yes.* What was in those little glass tubes, poison? *Yes.* Surely that knife hadn't been used in a murder, had it? *Yes.* And that gun, that piece of iron piping, that swordstick, that palm gun and—how on earth did the cuckoo clock get there?

It all went according to plan. Wylie was content to watch and listen and cup a whisky-and-soda in both hands, as if it was brandy. He watched, sleepy eyed. Jane's sleepiness was driven away, but she was a little uneasy. Esmeralda was so excited that she could hardly stop to sip her gin and Italian.

At last:

"Rolly, what on earth is that cuckoo clock doing there?"

"As a matter of fact," said Rollison easily, "it was a present from a French friend of mine. Nice of him, wasn't it? Instead of the cuckoo popping out while I stood in front of it and saw how it worked, the door opened and a bullet struck me between the eyes."

Esmeralda spun round, to stare aghast at his face.

"Not *really*? There's no scar. I—oh, you fool! But honestly, was there a bullet?"

"Yes."

After a long silence, Esmeralda took a longer sip of her drink than before, and then asked earnestly:

"How many people hate you like that, Rolly?"

"Oh, only one here and there."

"Quite enough, too," Wylie interpolated, to prove that he had not been asleep. "Mind if I get a word in edgeways, Es? Hrrrrmp. These—ah—exhibits, Rollison, are they all genuine?"

"John!" Jane Wylie's protest was almost anguished.

Rollison chuckled. "Fair question, after all the wall looks as phoney as a wall can be. But the answer's yes. Don't ask me why I started it, just be charitable because I was young when it really began. See that knife with the piece off the point? That was the first. An East Ender wanted for murder tried to stick that in my back, but thanks to my youth and inexperience, I was wearing a chain waistcoat. Ever seen one? There are still times when——"

"I have, yes," said Wylie, and he touched a small, glass case inside which there was a single silk stocking. It was crumpled and laddered—and one ladder had been stopped by a dab of scarlet nail varnish. "That doesn't really look lethal," Wylie added.

"Just an ordinary 15 denier with a few ladders," Rollison told him, "and it was worn by the last woman we hanged in this civilized country."

Wylie looked very bleak.

"I am opposed to hanging women," he said, and Esmeralda shuddered.

Jane Wylie looked at the stocking.

"Who was she?" Esmeralda asked.

"As a matter of fact," said Rollison, "she was as brave as any resistance hero; she was a beauty, and she died without naming the man who really sent her to the gallows. A man known as the Doc—an East End criminal who began a kind of protection racket among lesser thieves and fences. One of the fences fought back, when he was blackmailed. The Doc asked for five hundred pounds, threatening to give the police proof that the fence dealt in stolen goods, and——"

"Where did the girl come in?" interpolated Esmeralda.

Wylie watched Rollison closely; intently.

"She collected the money from the Doc's victims," Rollison said, "and this one said he knew who the Doc was and would give him away rather than pay a penny. To save her man, the girl killed the fence—and died for it."

Esmeralda breathed: "And this—this *beast* called the Doc let her die?"

"He couldn't have saved her," Rollison said practically. "He did try—he sent big sums of money to the best defending counsel in the country, but the evidence was too strong."

"What a sordid story," Jane Wylie said.

"Life, m'dear, life in the raw," declared Wylie.

"There's one thing you haven't told us," Esmeralda pointed out. "Why is the stocking here?"

"The fence who died had a queer idea that I'd help him against the Doc—and he'd sent for me. I arrived a few moments after the murder. The girl was getting through a window, and I held her by the legs. She was wearing those."

There was a deep quiet in the room.

Then, there came a sound which Rollison fancied he had heard before, a faint, distant whimper. Imagination.

"Rolly," asked Esmeralda, "what was her name?"

"Jessica Gay," said Rollison. "She came from a good home, and the Doc first ruined and then led her to the gallows. One day——"

The whimper came again. Imagination?

Rollison saw Jane Wylie glance towards the door, then at her husband, who appeared to have noticed nothing. The story of Jessica Gay seemed to have shocked him deeply.

"*Ya*," came the sound, more loudly and quite clearly. "*Ya, ah, ya, ah, ya.*"

This time, Wylie turned his head sharply, and Esmeralda looked at the door; and then back at Rollison. He was so startled that he was nonplussed, so completely unaware of the baby that he did not look even slightly ill-at-ease.

"*Ya-ah, ya-ah, ya.*"

The two women and John Wylie did not turn round this time, but continued to stare at Rollison; and it was well they did, or they would have missed the sight of a lifetime. One moment he stood staring almost foolishly at the door, the next he moved so swiftly that he seemed to be in two places at once. He reached the door but did not open it wide, just turned the handle and opened it an inch. Then he stood waiting, as if someone stood outside, ready to do him harm.

More clearly than before, and much more crossly, came the now familiar sound.

"*Ya, ah, ya, ah, ya, ah.*"

"That's a baby!" Jane Wylie exclaimed, and jumped up and made for the door.

"Stay there," said Rollison in a sharp, commanding voice, "stand still. All of you." And with one arm thrust out to check Jane Wylie's progress, he listened as if for other sounds.

3

THE MIND OF ESMERALDA

In the pause which followed and the tension which Rollison's manner had created, there sounded only the heavy breathing of John Wylie, and a kind of snuffling from the lounge hall. Then the snuffling stopped, but only to give way to a muffled crying.

Jane Wylie moved swiftly towards the door, in spite of Rollison.

"That's a *baby*!"

"That's right," agreed Rollison, "and I'm wondering where the stork is." He turned towards Jane and gave her a smile so bright and friendly and even gay that for a moment she was nonplussed too. "Give me another minute," he added, and moved with that startling speed to the other side of the door. He pressed close against the wall beyond, leaned forward for the handle, and pulled the door wide open.

The baby cried more loudly.

Beyond, there was gloom outside the range of light from this large room. The front door was closed, and Rollison looked at it tensely, as if he expected it to open, or else to find evidence that it was not properly closed. It was. He moved again, but this time with a difference; all his tension had gone. He flashed that smile again, taking in both Jane and Esmeralda, and said lightly:

"False alarm."

He went into the lounge hall, switching on the light. He could see every corner, every picture, every piece of furniture—and he saw the piece of paper held down by a glass paperweight on the writing bureau. Jane was hurrying towards him, with Esmeralda not far behind, but he reached the bureau and slipped the note into his pocket before anyone saw what he was doing. Then he went to the landing door and made sure that it was locked.

He turned round.

Jane and Esmeralda stood together just ahead of John Wylie, who was framed in the doorway. Both women looked about them, as if hunting some prey. Then Jane spotted two cushions out of place and moved towards the couch, while Esmeralda stepped to Rollison's side.

"So everything I've heard about you *is* true," she breathed.

Rollison, watching Jane, said mildly: "Mmmmm?" and then, realizing what she had said, turned to look sharply at Esmeralda. "What's that?"

"Everything *is* true," repeated Esmeralda. She looked at him with great green eyes shining, her lips parted, and her teeth glistening. She made a picture indeed.

"I don't get it," said Rollison, blankly. "What's true?"

"Your reputation," she cooed.

"Oh, that private eye nonsense——"

"I wasn't thinking about private eyes," said Esmeralda, "I was thinking about"—she hesitated, glanced towards the couch, and then said obscurely—"sailors." Satisfied, she turned and joined Jane, who was bending over the couch and moving one of the cushions.

There was the baby, enveloped in its grey shawl.

"Why, look!" exclaimed Esmeralda, "it can't be more than a week or two old!"

"No," said Jane, in a quiet, controlled voice, "two or three weeks at the most." She bent down and picked the baby up, slipping her hand round it protectingly, behaving as if this was the only tiny infant in the whole, wide world.

Esmeralda seemed to be infected with a gaiety which put a lilt into her voice and added brightness to her eyes.

"It looks healthy enough, anyhow; *look* at its fat cheeks." She did so for what seemed a long time, while Rollison busily contemplated her and the situation, and John Wylie watch him from the doorway. Then, slowly and with great deliberation, Esmeralda turned to look upon Rollison.

He had seldom undergone such an appraisal.

She was interested only in his face, and looked so long and lingeringly that it seemed almost as if she was dissecting it, feature by feature. Her eyes were still glistening, but her lips were pursed, as if she was bottling up some kind of merriment which might burst out any moment.

Then, she gravely shook her head.

"He isn't a bit like you," she announced, and turned back to Jane and the baby.

Jane was too interested in the child to hear what Esmeralda said; was fussing in a quiet way, unwrapping the grey shawl. But her husband heard, gulped, and said:

"Esmeralda, impertinent."

Esmeralda was not at all impressed by her uncle, but switched attention to the baby, touching pink cheeks, seeking tiny hands. Rollison stared ruefully at the girl as Wylie moved ponderously towards him, and said:

"Take no notice of her."

"No notice?" There was a moment's pause, and then Rollison grinned. "I certainly shall, that girl has a quick mind."

"Not offended?"

"If she means exactly what I think she means, I ought to feel highly complimented." Rollison said, and was relieved to see Wylie's stern face pucker into something near a smile. "Sadly, things are not always what they seem. Hold the fort for a few minutes, will you? Don't let anyone telephone." He went to the door, opened it, and bent down, studying the lock with great care. Wylie came towards him, interestedly. "Neat job," Rollison observed, "whoever did that is a craftsman and there aren't many of them to-day."

"Did what?"

"Broke in."

Rollison said that while getting up and dusting his knees, but Esmeralda spun round, her face ablaze with excitement, the baby quite forgotten.

"Rolly, is that what happened? Did someone break in here? Why, they might have——"

"Left a small atom bomb behind," said Rollison, and then chuckled. "Perhaps they did. Like to come with me, Esmeralda?"

"Where?"

"Looking for that stork."

"That what?" She was puzzled at first, then threw up her hands in delight. "Oh, I see!" She had never seemed more gay or wide awake, and it was now half-past three in the morning. "Where shall we look?"

"Downstairs, for a start." Rollison wasted no more time on her, but opened the bureau drawer and took out a flash-light, then went towards the landing door. Esmeralda was already there. He gripped her arm and squeezed, then said: "Give me half a minute, will you, there's something I want to do." He went ahead of her down the stairs, moving so fast that had she wanted to, she could not have caught up with him. He seemed to bound downwards like a spring uncoiling. Half-way down, he took out the pencilled note, and slackened his speed enough to read it; for this was what he wanted to do without Esmeralda's help.

It read:

The Doc's after the kid's mother and me.
If he gets a chance he'll snatch the kid.

That was all.

Rollison put the note back into his pocket as he reached

the ground floor. Esmeralda came floating down with a billow of black skirts and white lace and frills, for she was very feminine. She was equally eager. Rollison went to the front door, opened it, and shone his flashlight. Esmeralda bent down beside him.

"See that?" He pointed to scratches so faint that they were hardly visible. "The marks of his tool. He forced this lock and the one upstairs, left the baby, and——"

"*He* did?" Esmeralda's voice was shrill with doubt.

"If there's a woman in the world who could pick a lock like that, I'll freely admit that I'm the baby's father," Rollison said, and so robbed Esmeralda of all future chances of being sly and obscure. "I doubt if there are six men in London who could do it this way, without damaging the lock." He turned towards the street, where the darkness was greater now because only one other window showed any light, and the street lamps were a long way from Number 22. He shone the torch down on the steps leading to the front door, on to the pavement, on to the kerb. He stooped down, picked up a cigarette end, and took out his won cigarette case and put the end inside.

"Is that a clue?" breathed Esmeralda.

"Could be." Rollison behaved as if he had forgotten that she was there, and sprayed the kerb and the roadway with light. There was a damp dust in the gutter, and, just behind the Rolls-Bentley, tyre marks which no one could fail to see. He bent down closer, saying as if to himself:

"Very small tyre, either an old baby car or a motor-cycle, more likely motor-cycle. Pity Jolly isn't here, he could get a cast. Wonder if a flashlight photograph would show anything." He straightened up, fully aware of Esmeralda's closeness and her quick breathing. He was also aware of something else; a man turning into the street; but Esmeralda seemed to be unaware of that.

"Do you really think a flashlight photo——"

"*Shhhhh*," hissed Rollison, and gave her full value for her night out. "Someone's coming."

Esmeralda stood still and silent as a mouse, and did not even look away from Rollison. It would take a lot to make her jumpy; she had the steady nerves of healthy youth. As he glanced towards the corner he found himself thinking, absently, that there were more qualities in Esmeralda than he would have suspected while at the Star Club or on the way here.

Then: "It's all right," he said, "it's a policeman.

"A *copper*!"

"A policeman," repeated Rollison firmly. "We are in a mood to be polite. Start looking in front of the car, will you? Switch on the headlamps to give us more light."

Esmeralda didn't ask why, but obeyed. The big car's powerful lights showed more of the street than had been visible since dusk had fallen. The steady footsteps of the policeman drew nearer, while Rollison joined Esmeralda in the fake search.

The policeman drew level.

"Evening, sir." He looked down at Rollison, and on the instant his manner changed and his voice altered. "Good *even*ing, Mr. Rollison. Looking for something?"

Rollison straightened up.

"Hallo, Jim. Yes, I've lost a propelling pencil, no great value but sentimental, you know. Afraid it's not here, though—we've looked along the kerb pretty thoroughly."

"Perhaps it's under the car, sir."

"Could be," agreed Rollison, "but I don't think it's likely, I had it earlier in the evening. Probably left it at the Star Club. Serve me right if I will visit these dens of iniquity, doesn't it?"

"Oh, the *Star* Club is quite respectable, sir."

"It is?" Rollison sounded surprised. "I must have been misinformed." He waited for the policeman's chuckle, which wasn't long in coming, and sensed that Esmeralda was looking at him almost with awe. "Not a lot you don't know about your beat, Jim, is there?"

"Well," said the constable, modestly, "can't be sure that we keep track of everything, but since that burglary in

Gresham Mews we've been pretty much on the alert around here."

"I can imagine. Jim"—Rollison put a hand on Esmeralda's shoulder, and gripped firmly; warningly—"this is Miss Esmeralda Gale, and she doesn't know much about London by night. Earlier in the evening we were talking about your chaps on the beat, and I told her that there was very little you didn't notice if it was at all out of the ordinary."

"Well, sir, we're trained observers, you know."

"Believe me, I do! There was the time when—but never mind me," dissimulated Rollison hastily, "be a friend, and give us a demonstration."

"Well, sir——"

"Oh, *please*," begged Esmeralda.

"Well, don't hold me to everything, will you? I wouldn't swear to it all in the box, but I don't think there's much wrong. Let's see. I came on duty at eight o'clock, and at eight-twenty-seven there was a minor accident involving a car and a cycle, in which the cyclist received slight scratches and bruises of the right leg. There was a bit of thunder about. At eight-forty-three a high-powered car was heard to be moving very fast, probably considerably in excess of the speed limit, along Millaway Street towards Piccadilly Circus. At nine-ten there was a loud explosive noise coming from the direction of Hill Street, upon investigation this proved to be a window slamming as a result of a broken sash-cord, the breaking glass of which accounted for the explosive sound. We had quite a storm about then. At ten-nineteen a smell of smoke from the direction of . . ."

He went on, briskly and confidently, as if he were reporting to his sergeant. Esmeralda watched and listened, fascinated; and the constable, in his early thirties, was not at all bad-looking. Nor was he unaware of Esmeralda's gaze.

Rollison gave him full marks but wished that he would hurry; it would not be long before John or Jane Wylie came to investigate.

". . . at one o'clock, approximately, a two-stroke motor-cycle was heard to approach the vicinity from Piccadilly, and three or four minutes later the engine was switched off. Later, the motor-cycle was seen turning out of Gresham Ter—out of this *street*, sir, driven by a man with a female passenger——" the constable paused, grinned, and had second thoughts. "With a girl on the back. I personally checked every street door in the Terrace subsequent to that, sir, and every ground floor window. There was no indication of anything wrong. At two-o-three . . ."

Three minutes later, he finished, coughed, and looked mildly self-conscious; obviously he was even more aware of Esmeralda's glowing eyes.

"That was *won*derful," breathed Esmeralda, in a quivering voice, "it really was. Thank you very much indeed."

"Pleasure's mine, miss," the constable said. "Any time."

"From this night on I shall sleep sounder whenever I know you're on duty, Jim," Rollison said, and proffered cigarettes. "I know you can't smoke now, but that's a large helmet you're wearing." The constable scooped, gratefully. "Now we'd better go and tell the others that we can't find the pencil," Rollison said to Esmeralda, "or they'll think we've eloped. Good night." He took Esmeralda's arm firmly and led her away, and the policeman did not move until the door had closed on them. "Esmeralda," went on Rollison with deep feeling, "you could be the ruin of that young man's life."

"Rolly darling," cooed Esmeralda, "I don't care how many babies there are, I think you're a genius. No wonder you're so famous! That couple on the motor-cycle *did* bring the baby here, didn't they?"

"It's possible."

"And the way you wormed it out of the policeman was absolutely gorgeous," went on Esmeralda, marvelling. By then, they were half-way up the stairs. "Without giving him the faintest idea that anything had happened here, too.

Of course I can understand why you mustn't allow anyone to learn about this," she continued, becoming earnest and conspiratorial. "You needn't worry about me. I'll keep mum, but you might find it difficult with John and Jane. Especially Jane. She has rather a thing about there being one law for the rich and one for the poor, you know, and the fact that it would cause a dreadful scandal and get in all the newspapers if it leaked out, wouldn't stop her. You're going to have your work cut out to convince her that the baby isn't yours," declared Esmeralda, "that's about the only way you'll keep her quiet. Jane's a wonderful Aunt and I'm very fond of her, but she's got such an uncomfortable *conscience*."

Rollison looked thoughtfully down upon the golden head.

"Whereas you just have a mind," he observed. "I wouldn't like to be the man who marries you, my Esmeralda. Now let's go and do battle with Aunt Jane."

As they went up, he wondered a little uneasily how right Esmeralda was about her aunt.

4

SWEET REASON

SIR JOHN WYLIE, looking more blackly massive than ever, smoking a pipe and so providing a screen for his red-rimmed, tired eyes, was by himself in the living-room-cum-study. There was no sign of Jane or the baby. From the direction of the bedroom, which was approached from a passage leading to the kitchen and bathroom, there came the faint sound of crooning; it was the first lullaby that had ever been heard in Rollison's flat.

"Hallo," Rollison greeted, "is your wife playing mother?"

"That's about it," said Wylie, and took out his pipe and pointed it at Esmeralda. "Go and see if you can help her." No Victorian father could ever have been more emphatic with a daughter whom he wanted out of earshot, and for some reason best known to herself, Esmeralda went off meekly. Wylie put the pipe back between his full lips, and regarded his host through a grey haze of smoke. Then he said: "Hmm."

"You could be more explicit," murmured Rollison.

"I am trying," announced Wylie, heavily. "Man of few words y'know. Very ticklish situation. My wife"—he pondered, chewing the stem of his pipe, and then he struck oil—"believes right's right," he finished.

"Hear, hear," approved Rollison.

"No joking matter," Wylie said. "She's outraged."

"Not, I trust, literally."

"Positively. Very difficult situation for me," went on Wylie. "Embarrassing. Fact is, Jane——"

"Let me try to make it a little easier for you," suggested Rollison kindly, "your wife can't imagine why anyone should dump a baby on my doorstep——"

"Couch."

"Couch, if we must be literal."

"Important difference," declared Wylie.

Rollison looked baffled and felt baffled. It was as if he had been fighting against unknown forces from the moment he had agreed to bring this little party here. Had he come alone, had he discovered the sleeping infant himself, it would have been bad enough, and the pencilled note would not have made it any easier; but if the situation wasn't quickly corrected, it could get out of hand. Wylie's erratic manner of speech did nothing to help, and whenever Rollison thought of Esmeralda it was a little uneasily, for there was old devil mischief in the child. Child?

It would be easy for Rollison to lose patience; but not wise.

"Where is the important difference?" he asked patiently.

"Doorstep, couch."

"I was speaking figuratively."

Wylie contemplated him as if he, not Wylie, was being obtuse.

"My wife is a literal woman," he announced, at last. "No kinder-hearted woman in the world, but—never mind. Literal, logical and highly intelligent. A baby on the doorstep is one thing. No key required. A baby on the couch in a locked apartment—key required." Wylie paused as if for breath, and Rollison waited, admiration mingling with apprehension. "Who would have a key?" inquired Wylie, and then made almost desperate circles in the air with his pipe. "No offence meant," he blurted and as if to protect himself against any further indiscretion, he put the pipe back in his mouth.

Rollison studied him.

It was easy to fill in the gaps in Wylie's dissertation, and obvious that he and Jane had been busily talking for much of the time that Rollison and Esmeralda had been downstairs. Put bluntly and simply, the Wylies had jumped to the conclusion that no one would present Rollison with a child, without good reason: that probably the child was his.

The difficulty was to stop his lips from twitching.

He could soon disabuse the Wylies; the pencilled note would be enough for anyone who was literal-minded. But at this stage, did he want to disabuse them? The note was a plea, and the note had mentioned 'The Doc'. This was the first time he had heard of the Doc since his return from New York, but he knew that many people, little crooks and honest men alike, were in terror of him.

Someone unknown had brought the infant, apparently believing with a startling faith that he, Rollison, would protect it.

And the Doc might snatch, might kidnap the child.

If the Doc knew where it was, if he suspected that it had been brought to this flat, it would be easy for him to find out where it was being cared for; so a snatch would be possible if not easy.

The fewer to know where the baby was, the safer.

For the time being, Rollison decided, the important thing was to keep the Wylies quiet; for the truth might make them talk, or make them insist on bringing in the police, and if the writer of the note had wanted that, he would have gone to the police himself.

All these things passed through Rollison's mind as he studied John Wylie's heavy features. So did Esmeralda's opinion of Jane Wylie's character. Esmeralda was probably ignorant of one thing because she was very young. Among people of the Wylies' generation—which was also Rollison's—there was a kind of code. A high moral conviction might possess Jane, making her believe that he must 'do right' by the mother; but she would give him the chance to do so before trying to exert any pressure—such as threatening to gossip about the new arrival at Gresham Terrace.

Now Rollison believed that he needed a little straight man-to-man stuff with Wylie.

"Wylie," he said slowly, "I don't mind admitting that all this is a shock. Big one, too. Caught me on the wrong foot, so to speak. I know I can rely on your discretion. Your wife's too. I need just a little time to—er—make arrangements. I shan't let anyone down, of course."

Out came the pipe and, explosively: "Of course not! Regret, personally, we decided to come here. Very interesting trophy wall, though." Wylie's eyes did not twinkle and his face did not light up, but he did not need to add that the most interesting trophy was the one collected to-night. "I'll have a word with Jane. Ah—'nother problem."

Oh, *no*!

"Oh?"

Wylie jerked the stem of the pipe towards the bedroom.

"Needs woman's care," he announced.

"Ah," said Rollison very softly, and had one of his better moments. "You couldn't be more right. Do you think that your wife——?"

"Surprised if she won't," declared Wylie. "Might be an idea if you went along now—see how things are." Back went the pipe, this time with finality, and he moved away towards his chair and a glass which was still half full of whisky and soda.

Rollison put a cigarette to his lips, and stepped slowly towards the bedrooms. There were two at this side of the flat, his—which was large—and a spare one which was much smaller. He had taken it for granted that Jane was in his room, but soon realized that he was wrong. The light showed at the door of the spare room.

That was unfortunate, but Rollison found himself smiling as he tapped at the door. If ever two were available to add to two, it was here. By accident—it was hard to believe that it was design—Jane had gone into this room. She would have looked about for things she needed for the baby, and would have found women's clothes in the wardrobe, make-up in the dressing-table, a room that was much more boudoir than one would expect in any bachelor's flat.

Rollison went in.

Esmeralda, her eyes still glistening and a kind of awe in her expression, stood by the dressing-table. Jane Wylie was sitting on the edge of a large single bed. The clothes had been turned down and the baby, still in the shawl, lay on it like a huge grey chrysalis. Pillows on either side were placed so that it could not roll off. Jane, frowning, looked up. She was a handsome woman and there was no doubt that she had a conscience: it seemed to be written in her eyes.

"Jane," said Rollison, firmly, "I'm in a bad spot, you don't need telling that, and I need a little time to sort things out. If I ask my family or my friends for help, gossip will go on wings, and before I know where I am, the newspapers will get this story. So they will if I try to put the child in a nursing home. Will you come to my rescue?"

Straight Jane looked at him squarely.

"I don't see why I should."

"Nor do I, but will you?"

Esmeralda was handling a gold framed hand mirror, the back worked with beautiful *petit point*, and looking at herself in it. She glanced at Jane, but didn't speak; she knew when silence was called for.

"Someone has to look after the baby, I suppose," Jane said practically. "I'd better have a word with John. I'll look after him for the night, anyhow; I certainly shan't leave him here."

Rollison gulped. "Him?"

Jane raised her hands. "Do you seriously mean to say you didn't know what sex——" she broke off, jumped up, and pushed past him angrily.

When her voice was audible in the big room, Esmeralda looked seductively into Rollison's eyes, and said cooingly:

"Isn't this a beautiful dressing table set?"

"Yes, isn't it?"

"And what a lovely room."

"Beautiful."

"You know, Rolly, I've been thinking," declared Esmeralda. She put the mirror down, and picked up a tiny scent spray and pressed the bulb gently. She half closed her eyes, as if in ecstasy. "A lot of people call you Rolly, a few call you Richard, and of course everyone knows that you're called the Toff, but *I* have a new name for you."

"Oh." It was easy to be suspicious of this child. "What?"

"Lothario."

"One of these days I'm going to think up a new name for you," said Rollison, "and it won't be Calista. Esmeralda, I may need some help in the next day or two, and I'd want it from someone who knows about this, the fewer the better. Are you likely to be very busy?"

"Lothario," said Esmeralda, picking up the mirror and looking at herself again. She poked at her hair, put her head on one side, and at last seemed satisfied. "Lothario, if I can rely on an honorarium, say something like this, I'd be happy to help."

"And when it's over I shall recommend you strongly to one of the political parties; you'll be wasted outside the House of Commons. Are you staying with the Wylies?"

The look in Esmeralda's eyes was positively wicked.

"Yes, for a few days, but I share a flat in Shepherd Market; I can go back there whenever I like—I'm having a holiday on John and Jane. But you know! Shall I telephone you?"

"Please," said Rollison, and rounded the bed and took the mirror away from her. "This is to be for a mission accomplished, not for promised help."

"I'll remember," Esmeralda said.

Twenty minutes later, Rollison saw them all into the Rolls-Bentley, Jane in the back this time carrying the baby, Esmeralda sitting next to Wylie. The car moved off with only a whisper of sound, and as its red light disappeared, Rollison turned and hurried upstairs, to come back again within five minutes, carrying a camera with a special lens and a flashlight. Jolly, his man, was an accomplished amateur, and his equipment was always in the flat. Rollison bent down and focused, and a bright flash lit up the street —once, twice. Going back into the house, he wondered if Jim the policeman had noticed the flashes and was already on his way to investigate.

That didn't matter.

He ran up to the flat, closed the door and went straight to the telephone. He dialled an East End number, and after a long pause, a man answered in a sleepy voice.

"Whossat?"

"Bill," said Rollison, "I'm sorry to worry you now, but could you send a couple of men to Throgmorton Square for me?"

There was a pause.

Ebbutt, the man at the other end of the line, was an old friend of the Toff, a man of influence in the East End, and of many parts. He had often done such things as this—but now his hesitation seemed very marked.

Then: "What's the trouble, Mr. Ar?"

"I just want a house watched—there's a possible baby-snatch in the offing."

"Oh," said Ebbutt. "Sure, okay, Mr. Ar. I'll fix it. What's the number of the 'ouse?"

He did not sound as enthusiastic as he often had in the past, but Rollison put that down to his being woken out of a heavy sleep.

Rollison pushed the telephone away, lit a cigarette and poured himself another brandy and soda. He sat back in an armchair facing the trophy wall, and closed his eyes, but he had seldom been further from sleep at four o'clock in the morning.

The Doc was putting on the black again—so much seemed obvious, but that wasn't the matter of first importance. The man who had forced these locks held pride of place.

Rollison knew that strata of London known as the 'underworld' almost as well as the most knowledgeable officials at Scotland Yard; and one by one he conjured up mental images of men who could force locks as expertly as his had been forced.

He narrowed the number down to seven. Two of these he ruled out because they were old, and not likely to have a vested interest in a baby and certainly not likely to ride about on a motor-cycle. Two more he ruled out because he knew that they were in jail. That left him with three.

Suddenly, he opened his eyes wide, finished his drink, and jumped up.

"I'll check with the Yard in the morning," he told himself, "and then get busy. There probably isn't more than one motor-cycling safebreaker."

He was humming to himself as he went into the bathroom—and then he stopped abruptly. In the bath were damp-looking babies' napkins, and from the towel rail a towel was missing.

"And practical too," he said, laughed, spread another towel over the heap of soggy napkins, and began to brush his teeth.

He was on the point of getting into bed, at twenty minutes to five, when the telephone bell rang.

5

FEAR BY PHONE

THERE was a telephone at the side of Rollison's bed, but he was so awkwardly placed that he could not get at it quickly, and it gave four more sharp bursts of ringing before he could lift the receiver. By then he was sitting on the side of the bed, in front of a large dressing-table mirror, which showed his hair standing on end after the scramble to answer the call.

"Richard Rollison here," he said.

There was no answer.

"Hallo, there. This is Richard Rollison."

There was no answer, but there were sounds, a kind of hissing noise, one that he associated with someone out of breath. It seemed close to the mouthpiece, and came very clearly.

"Hallo," he said, very distinctly and sharply.

Then, a woman's voice came.

"Is—is that—is that the Toff?"

The voice was very faint, but unmistakably a woman's. There was nothing special about it, except a trace of Cockney in the last word, making 'Toff' sound almost 'Torf'. Yet the manner of her speaking told him much more than the words, for it spoke of fear. Fear and a breathless woman and a call so early in the morning.

"Yes," he said carefully, "this is the Toff. Can I help you?"

Silence.

This time, there was not even the hiss of agitated breathing, only the stillness. He had heard no sound of the receiver being replaced, or being dropped. He held on, no longer speaking, looking at the dial on his telephone and wishing for the days of manual exchanges, when it would have been easy to trace this call.

A motor horn brayed a clear warning. It must be very close to the telephone at the other end, which placed it as a telephone kiosk call near a road. He heard other sounds, and fancied that one was of someone running.

The woman spoke again, urgently.

"Why don't you answer, is that——"

"This is the Toff speaking. Who——"

She cut right across his words.

"Listen, mister, look after my baby, *please*! Make sure he has a good home." Now, the woman cried. "They're going to kill me, I'm sure they're going to——"

"Stop a moment!" said the Toff with sudden and sharp vehemence, and so made her break off. "Listen carefully now. Give me your name and tell me exactly where you are."

"I—I don't know that I can, I——" there was another pause, another voice in the background. It wasn't possible to be sure whether the second voice was hostile or friendly; it was just that of a man speaking quickly, using words which Rollison couldn't distinguish, although he caught: 'Get a move on.' Then there was a new sound, the last Rollison wanted to hear just then; the clatter as the receiver was banged down.

He put his down, slowly.

The frightened woman might be anywhere in London—anywhere within the London dialling district, and the kiosk might be any one of several thousand. Rollison sat quite still, looking at his reflection without noticing his set expression or, for that matter, his royal blue pyjamas. A frightened woman with a slightly Cockney voice, a desperate mother, a man who had left the baby and the note about the Doc. Add it all up. Add it all up, yes, and look for the thing he hadn't yet seen, something which was on the edge of his mind, something he had missed. It was that faculty, of being sensitive to factors he knew existed but couldn't place, which made him what he was.

Suddenly, he snapped his fingers.

"Didn't hear her press Button A," he said, and immediately lifted the receiver, "so it might not have been a dial call." He dialled 'O', asked for the telephone supervisor, and found her helpful and quick.

". . . yes, that's right, sir, there was a call to your number from Guildford, about five minutes ago. It will take a few minutes to get further particulars, if you would care to hold on——"

"I won't hold on," said Rollison in his friendliest voice, "but if you'll find out where the call came from, also getting the address if possible, I'll call you back."

"If it's a private number, sir, I shall not be allowed to disclose any information except the number."

"That's all right," Rollison said. "I'll call back in ten minutes."

He rang off again, and sat quite still until he stretched out for a cigarette, and lit it slowly.

He could call Scotland Yard, and be reasonably sure that they would help; but they would also be curious. Did he want the police to be curious, yet? He couldn't escape from one piece of reasoning; that if the parents of the child had thought that the police could help, they would have called on them. *Add it up*. A man who could pick locks like this one wasn't likely to have many friends among or liking for the police, even if the Doc was putting pressure on him. If he had a record, as was probably the case, he would want to keep away from authority—more especially if he was on the run.

Rollison looked at himself in the mirror, and put his head on one side.

"You are slipping," he announced. "Of course they're on the run, and they hadn't anywhere to park the baby. Not much chance of getting away from the police while carrying an infant of that age, so——"

What of the woman's fear?

If this had been planned cold-bloodedly, if parents simply wanted to be free from the child, would the woman have sounded so frightened? And remember the talk of the Doc.

Rollison reached a decision.

He lifted the receiver again, and dialled Whitehall 1212. When a brisk-voiced operator said: "Scotland Yard," he asked at once:

"Superintendent Grice isn't there by any chance, is he?"

"No, sir, I'm afraid not."

"Chief Inspector Worley?"

"No, sir."

"Chief Inspector Knott?"

"Yes, sir, he's in his office. Who shall I tell him is calling?"

"Richard Rollison."

"Richard Rol——" echoed the operator, and then stopped abruptly, only to go on in a different tone: "Mr. Rollison, yes sir. I'll put you through at once."

"Thanks very much," said Rollison warmly.

Knott was a youngish man, only recently promoted, and was particularly well-disposed, because a few months earlier he had arrested a murderer in what was generally accepted as a very smart piece of work; hence his promotion. He was well aware that he would not have made the arrest but for the Toff, and was not likely to stand on ceremony.

"Hallo, Rollison, can't you sleep?" Knott had a lively voice. "What's the trouble?"

"It's my guilty conscience and a curious telephone call," said Rollison mildly.

"Can't do anything about your conscience," said Knott; it was easy to imagine his grin. "What information do you want about the telephone call?"

"The number in Guildford, hence the address," Rollison told him. "The Supervisor is getting both, but won't confide in an ordinary humble citizen. If I tell her to refer to the Yard, she might decide to trust me."

"And she might also check with us," said Knott dryly. "All right, you can give us as a reference. What's it all about?"

"When I've found out, I'll tell you."

"I hope you mean that! How did the American trip go, by the way? I read bits and pieces about you; you seem to have taken New York by storm."

"In fact they took me by the seat of my pants, but I survived," said Rollison, and took advantage of Knott's expansive mood. "The trouble is that I'm out of touch over here, just now."

"Exactly what else do you want to know?"

Rollison chuckled.

"Go on like this, and I'll begin to think you earned your promotion after all! What kind of a reputation has the Doc won for himself lately?"

There was a long pause, so long that it seemed ominous. Then at last:

"Nasty," said Knott, and his voice sharpened noticeably. "There was another ugly killing in Shadwell five weeks ago, not much doubt that the Doc did it, or else he was behind it. We didn't put an end to him when we hanged Jessie Gay. Is this——"

"Know who he is, yet?"

"No."

"We must find out," said Rollison, earnestly. "Chief Inspector, I can't thank you enough, and if anything happens that is likely to interest you, I'll pass it on."

"Mind you do," said Knott. He did not sound quite so amiable now; mention of the Doc had obviously troubled him. "Take my advice, and make sure what you're doing before you tackle anything that the Doc's involved in. He's reputed to have said he'll break you, for catching Jessie Gay."

"Oh, *has* he?" said Rollison heavily. That woman's fear had been real fear, remember. "I'll be very careful indeed," he promised. "Good-bye."

He rang off, stubbed out the cigarette, which he had drawn at only three or four times, and called the exchange again. The Supervisor was obviously waiting for him, and when he referred her to Scotland Yard, she said at once:

"I don't think that will be necessary, I'll just put a note on my report, Mr. Rollison." So she had been busy, and had identified him. Bless his reputation! "The call came from Guildford 05691, and the name and address of the subscriber is Robertson, Rose Cottage, Horsham Road."

"You're very good," Rollison said, "thank you very much indeed."

She gave a little, self-conscious laugh.

"It's a pleasure to help the Toff, sir!"

Rollison chuckled as he rang off; spontaneous tributes such as that did a great deal for his ego. He went back into the bathroom, doused his face in cold water, then dressed very quickly. He was outside in less than ten minutes, striding along Gresham Terrace to the mews round the corner; there, he kept his car, to-day a scarlet Bristol. As he was backing it out of the garage, the policeman to whom he had talked earlier passed the end of the mews, and made a point of calling out.

"Up early, sir?"

"Candle at both ends, Jim, it'll be the death of me," Rollison said, and waved.

Dawn was breaking, but it was still quite dark. A few buses, menacing in their speed along the empty roads, were coming in from the suburbs. Small vans and one or two donkey-drawn carts, piled high with fruit and vegetables, were coming away from the city; doubtless from Covent Garden. Cyclists had their coats buttoned high to the neck, and put down their heads as protection against the cutting October wind.

Rollison drove almost sedately until he had crossed Putney Bridge, where the dawn began to silver both the sky and the river. Then he put on speed. He knew Guildford well, and did not need to ask the way in the cobbled High Street, but turned on to the Horsham Road at once. Then he slowed down. Rose Cottage might be in the centre of the town, or else a mile or two along. He saw a postman cycling, pulled up alongside and asked:

"Which direction is Rose Cottage, do you know?"

"Straight along, sir, almost the last house in Guildford, that is—right on the corner, you can't miss it. The road's very narrow there, and there's a halt sign."

"That's fine," said Rollison. "Thanks." He drove on, speeding again, but feeling more tired than he had all night; there was a stinging sensation at the back of his eyes. Now, he was inclined to scoff at himself, for this was almost certain to be a wasted journey. Then recollection of the woman's scared manner and of the sudden silence drove thought of wasted time away. It was about an hour since the woman had telephoned; he could not have come more quickly, and he might conceivably be in time to help.

He followed a bend in the road, and saw Rose Cottage. He couldn't mistake the way the road narrowed, or the big warning HALT sign, the white lines on the road. The red brick cottage had probably been there for three hundred years, and nearly every motorist who had to drive past it thought that it ought to have been torn down in the early days of motoring. It was low-roofed, the roof itself was bent and crooked, the red tiles were touched with the green of lichen. Small windows fronted the road, and the front door opened straight on to the road; as dangerous as it could be. There was a wooden gate to a small, hedged garden and a back door. A few yards this side of the cottage was a bay where he could park, and a notice: *J. Robertson Builder and Decorator*. He pulled the car in and sat for a moment, stiff after the journey and his night without sleep.

"What I need now is a cup of strong coffee," he said aloud. He got out, lit a cigarette, and approached the wooden gate. Near it was a layer of thin, damp dirt—and across this was a tyre track which he recognized on the instant; that of the motor-cycle which had been in Gresham Terrace.

"Now we shouldn't be long," he said softly, and went into the garden.

Everything near the cottage was quiet, only the birds in the hedges and the nearby trees made any noise, and he hardly noticed them. He was studying the brick path which led to the back door, seeing footsteps in the damp earth on either side of the path—the footsteps of big men.

The lace curtains at the small windows were drawn. These, and something about the house itself, made him think of old people. On a line at the back hung a pair of men's long, woollen pants and of women's combinations; undoubtedly an old couple lived here.

By the back door was a window where the curtain was pulled a little to one side, so that he could see in. He glanced through the window, wondering what excuse he should give for waking anyone up so early; if this really was early, in the country. The cottage, the hanging clothes, the little patch of vegetable garden, the shed in the garden with builder's ladders and a builder's hand cart, all had a quiet, peaceful look.

Then, all thought of peacefulness fled.

An old woman, her grey hair spread out on a dark floor, lay in a huddled heap in the doorway of the room.

6

DEATH FOR TWO

ROLLISON moved swiftly away from the window, and reached the small back door. Its iron knob was shiny black, the big hinges fastened to the heavy oak were painted, too; and the panels had been freshly oiled. He pushed the door with his shoulder, but it didn't budge. There might be prints on the handle. He took out a handkerchief, then breathed on the knob, and saw several prints; he gripped where he would smear none, and turned the handle.

The door opened smoothly and silently.

His shadow was cast into the small kitchen, and over the woman lying half-way inside the room, half-way in a room beyond. There was a slight smell of gas. The woman lay so still that she seemed to speak of death.

Rollison closed the door, and then went down on one knee.

The grey hair was loose on one side, fluffy and almost white; one or two metal curlers held it tight on the other side. One arm was hidden by her body, the other lay twisted at an odd angle. She was short and plump. Her legs thrust out of the bottom of an old woollen dressing gown, one foot bare, the other still covered with a knitted slipper. The blue knots of varicose veins showed on the right leg.

Rollison took her hand, and tested the pulse, but felt nothing of life.

He took his forefinger away, and then tried again; but there was no beat at all. Very gently, he moved her so that he could see her face. Then he saw what had killed her. There were bruises at her throat, and scratches too; someone had choked the life out of her, and left her there like an empty sack.

He got up, and went into the room beyond, a living-room and parlour, crammed with Victorian furniture, the walls filled with sepia photographs and, on one, the photograph of a man in a private's uniform of the first World War, with service medals beneath it. The telephone was on the inside ledge of the window. Another door led out of this room and Rollison went to it. Beyond was a flight of stairs on one side, and the front door of the cottage on the other. He walked up the narrow stairs, bending his head because the ceiling was so low. The stairs creaked, uneasily. He reached a landing, which was just a square yard between two doors, both of which stood open. The first was a single bedroom, with a sloping roof, a tallboy and other oddments of furniture. The other was a larger bedroom with a double bed, and on the bed an old man, clearly the man of the photograph downstairs.

He had been strangled, too.

Rollison spent ten minutes looking round the cottage, and found little that helped, unless it was a photograph of a fair-haired girl and a dark-haired youngster which had the name of a Whitechapel photographer on the back. There were some letters, written in a neat handwriting but badly spelt, always signed:

Your ever loving Evie

Then a glance through the letters told a story, with phrases like: "I'll be glad when it's here, now," and "I wonder if it will be a boy, Dan says it's got to be!" making the story crystal clear. Dan and Evie and a baby on the way—and the last of these letters was dated four weeks earlier.

Tucked inside the envelope, so that Rollison nearly missed it, was a telegram:

It's a boy, both doing well, Dan

Proud parents; proud grandma, proud grandpa.

When Rollison left the cottage, closing the door softly behind him, his lips were set tightly and in his eyes was an angry, savage look.

The scarlet Bristol turned off the Embankment, bright in sparkling sunshine, crunched through leaves of the plane trees brought down by the night's wind, and pulled up outside the main C.I.D. building. Two or three policemen saluted Rollison, no one questioned him until he was up in the hall, where the sergeant on duty, a white-haired man who had served here before the Toff had been born, looked at him with a smile which suddenly disappeared.

" 'Morning, sir. Want Mr. Grice?"

"Please."

"He asked you to go straight up, sir."

"Thanks." Rollison nodded and forced a smile and then hurried along the wide corridors to the stairs; he did not want to be caught in the lift with amiable C.I.D. men who had fun in ribbing the Toff. He reached Grice's door, tapped, and started to open it on Grice's "Come in". This was a smallish room, with two wide windows overlooking the Embankment, Grice's big desk and a smaller one, which was empty. Grice was tall, spare and hollow-cheeked. His sallow skin seemed to stretch too tightly over his nose, making the bridge white and sharp, and over his chin, making that look sharp and pointed. He had fine brown eyes, was dressed in brown, and had thinning brown hair with hardly a trace of grey.

He started with a dry, almost laconic greeting and a sardonic grin.

"Hallo, Rolly, don't say New York's taught you how to hurry. I——"

He broke off as he rounded the desk, shook hands, and then said quietly:

"What's as bad as this?"

"Bill," said Rollison, "I could go out and do murder myself."

"My advice would be not to."

Rollison grave a frosty grin. "I might even follow it." He paused only for a moment. "I know you can't make any firm promises, but if it's possible, I want you to keep me right out of this affair for a few days, anyhow. I'll make the reason clear as I talk."

"I'll do what I can. Sit down, and——"

"Mind if I stand?" Rollison meant if he walked, for he began to pace the room as he started the story. He left nothing out, and put nothing in that had no direct bearing on the crimes. He watched Grice become more and more serious and grim, saw him making notes on a slip of paper. Grice didn't once interrupt.

As he finished, Rollison said:

". . . if the Doc knows that the baby was brought to me, he'll probably find out where the baby is now. I don't want to take that chance. So it's better if he doesn't even guess that I'm involved."

"No need to bring you into it at all," said Grice. "I'll call Guildford, and have them go and have a look at Rose Cottage." He didn't add that Rollison should have reported before, just put in the call. While waiting, he went on:

"You know that the Doc hates your guts, don't you?"

"I've only heard a little."

"You'll soon hear more. Jessica Gay was hanged after you'd left England and the Doc spread a whispering campaign that you'd never come back to the East End, that he'd make it so hot for you that you wouldn't dare—and if you tried, he'd drive you out or cut your throat."

"I've heard that kind of talk before," Rollison said.

"Take it seriously this time," Grice advised, soberly. "As you'd caught Jessie Gay, there was a stiffening attitude towards the Doc, and a lot of men defied him. That was partly because they believed you'd help them when you came back. So the Doc was quiet for a month or so. When you didn't return as soon as expected he started again. The cold truth now," added Grice very grimly, "is that half the squeals we get come from the Doc. He makes the crooks and fences pay him protection money, or he shops them. We have to act on the information, but at times it makes us sick. We'd far rather put the Doc inside than——"

Grice stopped, abruptly.

"I see exactly what you mean," Rollison said quietly, "and I suppose this could be a wily way to get at me. But if so, why present me with that baby? Obviously the parents are terrified of the Doc, and——"

"Don't say I didn't warn you about him," Grice said.

"He's big, he's powerful, and he's got most of the East End boys scared. He uses every form of pressure—such as a threat to a newborn child. Now! What about this motor-cyclist and the woman? Know their names?"

"Eve and Dan," Rollison answered.

"Could be Daniel Rickett," Grice said at once, "he's the only Daniel who can pick a lock, as far as the records go. Lives in Whitechapel, number 17 Luke Street, I think—I'll check. I'm taking it for granted that nothing will stop you from going after the murderers."

Rollison, feeling and looking rather easier, said mildly: "Right in one. The murderers and the Doc. Is he really unknown?"

"We haven't once picked up a line to his real identity, or where he lives," Grice went on. "We do know that several of the older fences are already out of business, though, and the Doc's taken over. One of them is dead and buried."

"Murdered?"

"I think so," Grice went on grimly. "Rolly, let me give it to you as straight as I can. The Doc is one of the few men who, in twenty-five years, have really got both the big and the little crooks worried. He started off in the protection racket, but now we know that he buys stolen goods in a big way. We've picked up a few of his legmen, carrying stolen goods or money to pay for them, and we've tried to trace the goods back to the Doc, but the trail always peters out. We did get a squeal about ten weeks ago, but the squealer's body was pulled out of the Thames at Rotherhithe two days later. Like me to tell you something that will make you blush?"

"Impossible."

"We've often wished you were back. Only to-day the Assistant Commissioner asked whether I'd any objection to asking you if you'd care to have a look round for the Doc."

"That's taking fame too far," protested Rollison, righteously, but now that he had talked and now that he knew there would be no limit to the co-operation from the police, he felt much better. "Any leads you can spare?"

"Before we go into that, let me tell you this," Grice said. "You'll find that a lot of people you thought were your friends won't be friendly in the East End at the moment. You went abroad when there was trouble and the Doc put it around that he scared you off."

"Oh, did he," said Rollison heavily, and remembered Ebbutt's lack of enthusiasm. "I thought he'd run to earth, but——"

"Don't rely on anyone but yourself, don't trust a soul," Grice warned. "Now! We could give you a hundred leads, and they'd probably all fizzle out. Why don't you start with this baby business?" Grice gave a droll grin. "I've seen you at work often enough, and probably know one thing about you that you don't realize yourself."

"Several, probably, but which one?"

"To get results, you need a cause," said Grice. "You were born three centuries too late; a suit of armour, a trusty blade and a fair lady's reputation would have been exactly right for you."

"I've a cause this time," said Rollison, softly. "Do some things for me, Bill. Trace that motor-cycle, without letting it be known that you're after it. Find out if Dan Rickett and his wife are hiding out anywhere, but don't pull them in. Let me know if you find either of them dead, too."

Grice nodded, soberly.

"Just one other thing," added Rollison, and found himself able to smile. "Do you seriously think that to exert pressure on Rickett, the Doc would threaten Rickett's baby?"

"Yes," said Grice, abruptly, and glanced at the telephone as it rang. "That will probably be Guildford." He lifted the receiver. "Hallo? . . . Yes, he's here. For you," he added almost in the same breath, and held out the receiver.

Rollison moved towards him. "But no one knows I'm here."

Grice said: "That's what you thought."

Rollison took the receiver, hesitated, and said: "Richard Rollison speaking." He had no idea whom to expect, but for some reason he found himself thinking of Esmeralda and her round, pretty face and her wicked eyes. "Who——"

"So it's the ruddy Toff," a man said in a husky voice; the kind of voice it would be difficult if not impossible to identify. "Like some advice, Toff? Go back to the great U.S.A. Or go anywhere you like, so long as you don't start interfering in London; it isn't your territory any more."

Then he rang off.

Rollison looked at the receiver thoughtfully, replaced it with great deliberation, told Grice exactly what the man had said, and then added:

"And he sounded as if he believed it. How I hate these automatic exchanges——"

"I'll make sure it was a local call," Grice said, and picked up the receiver, asked the operator, and then put the receiver down and said: "It was."

"Bill, if that was the Doc and he doesn't want me to poach, he probably knows why I'm here," Rollison said. "If he's got the Ricketts, he may have made them tell where he left the baby." Now he stopped moving and speaking slowly, but quickened his pace towards the door. "The Wylies live in Throgmorton Square. Ebbutt's got a couple of men there, but it would be better to have one or two good plainclothes men keeping an eye on the place. Will you fix it? I'm going to my flat; the Doc's boys have probably paid me a visit, hoping to find the baby there."

He opened the door.

Grice was on his feet.

"I'll fix Throgmorton Square," he said. "That call wouldn't have been made if the Doc still had a man at your flat, but I'd better send someone with you, to——"

"Don't," urged Rollison. "If a friend of the Doc is waiting there I don't want him to think that a Yard man will follow me like Mary's lamb. He'll probably want to Teach Me A Final Lesson, and Warn Me Off the East End For Ever. So we'll let him try. Look after the Wylies and that baby. As soon as I'm through, I'll try to get a bodyguard there myself."

Grice was already at the telephone.

Rollison went downstairs much more quickly than he had come up. Two or three people greeted him, and he waved, but went on. The scarlet gleam of the Bristol streaked out of the gateway, accompanied by grins of the men on duty and the scowling drivers of three taxis and a bus who were all forced to brake. He went round Parliament Square, and heard Big Ben strike ten; just ten o'clock on a busy morning. St. James's Park and the Mall were empty; it wasn't until he reached Piccadilly that he had traffic troubles, and they didn't last very long.

He pulled up outside 22 Gresham Terrace, slammed the car door, and appeared to notice nothing; not even the two men in a saloon car which was parked near a corner. The street door was often open by day, and he left it open and hurried upstairs, whistling cheerfully. He took his time getting his keys out, while listening intently. He heard no sound from the flat, but did hear a sound below, probably in the hall.

The two men from the car?

He peered over the edge of the banisters, to see two heavily built men approaching the foot of the stairs.

He unlocked his own front door, opened it an inch or two, then closed it with an audible click, and started down the stairs. He kept close to the wall, so that the men would not be likely to see him until they were on the same flight of stairs.

7

FIRST ROUND

WHEN Rollison reached the landing of the next flight, he heard the faint sound of a footfall; that was all. He went to the side of the banister and peered cautiously into the well. He could see only one of the men, but could hear the other. The stealthiness of their movements surprised him, for surely they thought he was inside the flat—and safely out of earshot. It seemed almost as if they were waiting for something to happen.

Rollison went down another flight of stairs. Then he saw a head appear, followed by another. The men reached the landing below and started for the next flight, still very cautious. He was so placed that they couldn't yet see him. As they came into full view, he jumped at them. They first saw him in mid-air, only a few feet above them, and the shock was so great that they stood as if mesmerised. He was so near that he could almost touch them with his feet when one of them gave a gasping cry, and turned to run. The other thrust his right hand towards his pocket, obviously going for a weapon, but he had no time to get it. Rollison crashed into him, bowling him over, and the man groaned as he toppled backwards. Rollison, his own fall broken, twisted to one side but couldn't save himself from falling, too. He saw several things happen at once.

The man who had turned to run was still on the move, now at the foot of this flight of stairs, turning and looking over his shoulder. He had one hand thrust outwards, as if to save himself from banging into the wall. The man on this landing hit the back of his head against the floor with a crunching thud; then he lay still, arms and legs flopping down. A gun poked out of his coat pocket, obviously that was what he had been trying to get.

If one man was armed——

Rollison rolled over, reaching for the gun. He saw the man at the foot of the stairs swing round, saw the gun in his hand, too. There was a sharp hiss of sound, and Rollison flopped on to his stomach. He thought he heard a humming sound of a bullet but it might have been imagination. He levelled the gun he had taken, and squeezed the trigger; the recoil was sharp, but the sound very subdued. He heard the bullet strike the wall below; then there was a gasp. Still on his stomach, head towards the top of the stairs, he wriggled forward to peer down.

The other man below was closer to the next flight of stairs than he had been. He held his gun cocked, but didn't look as if he enjoyed the idea of a duel. He caught sight of Rollison and fired again as Rollison took another shot at him.

"With love to the Doc," Rollison said, "but don't add any kisses."

The man below him darted back out of sight, and odd little sounds suggested that he was on his way down. Rollison got to his feet and moved to a spot from which he could see the hall. The man appeared close to the wall, peering upwards. He was heading for the front door, and there was little likelihood that he would come back alone.

Rollison fired again. A bullet smacked into the floor not a foot away from the other's foot. As it did so, the man leapt desperately for the street door, which was ajar. He didn't close the door as he rushed out.

Rollison relaxed, drawing the back of his hand across his forehead; he was wet with cold sweat. Then he eased his collar, dabbed at his neck, and slipped the gun into his pocket. Next he studied the unconscious man, who had fallen just clear of the hair carpet, and struck the stone floor. The blow might have put him out for ten minutes, or he might come round at any moment; and people from the other flats might come up or down the stairs.

"I hate to do it," Rollison said. "I'd much rather make you walk."

He bent down, hoisted the man to his shoulders, and straightened up. He staggered, but kept upright. Now and again he rested on the way up, but he reached the landing outside his front door without disaster. He was breathing very hard, and thinking harsh things about the soft life he had been living, when he felt his victim's body stiffen.

The man was coming round.

Rollison let him slide to the ground, then supported him against the wall. Two old folk had been choked to death, and this man's hands might be the hands which had done the choking. They were big and powerful. He wasn't fully conscious yet, but his eyelids were flickering, and he was able to stand upright. Rollison was grateful for the respite, and the chance to get his breath back. He took out a cigarette but didn't light it, and he waited for understanding to dawn in the other's eyes.

Those eyes opened very wide, and for the first time the man appeared to realize what had happened. He opened his mouth, and closed it again, abruptly. He squared his shoulders, looked right and left, towards the head of the stairs and then towards the unlocked door, which was within hand's reach of him.

He seemed to go stiff with fear.

"Good morning," said Rollison politely. "Quite chilly, isn't it?"

He wasn't surprised when the man reared up, turned, and flung himself towards the stairs. Rollison promptly put out his right foot; the other tripped over it and fell headlong, this time hitting the floor with his forehead.

"First the back and then the front; you're making quite a job of it," murmured Rollison. "But as you work for the Doc, he'll probably patch you up. If he ever sees you again, of course." He grinned almost inanely as the other began to get to his feet. "That will depend on the little chat we're going to have."

The man was now on his knees; swaying.

"You can do better than that," encouraged Rollison, "get straight up and step right into my parlour."

The man licked his lips; and there was terror in him.

He was as tall as Rollison, which meant that he stood over six feet. He was very broad, and looked very powerful. His face was ruddy-hued, as if he lived an outdoor life, and there was little doubt of his physical strength. There was nothing ugly or uncouth about him; his features were quite good, and he wasn't bad-looking.

But he was terrified.

That might be partly due to shock at coming round and finding himself a prisoner. Whatever the reason, the fear was there.

Frightened men often talked freely.

"After you," invited Rollison, and extended his hand towards the door.

The man said: "I—I—no! Don't——"

"But I insist," said Rollison earnestly, "*toujours la politesse* and all those continental gallantries. Inside." He took the man's right arm and propelled him towards the door—and met a weight of resistance he hadn't expected. Fifteen stone of flesh, bone and blood leaned heavily against him, as if in desperation.

"No! Don't—don't go in there!"

"I assure you that it's quite habitable," Rollison said, "in fact it's fairly comfortable, even though you aren't likely to experience——" He paused. "*What* did you say? 'I won't', or 'don't'?"

There was the fear, naked fear on the big face and in the pale grey eyes.

"I—I—I——" the man began, and then he wrenched himself free and dashed for the stairs again, as if he could sweep Rollison and all opposition aside. Rollison stopped him with a short arm jab to the stomach, then gripped his right arm again and pulled it behind him and thrust it upwards in a hammer-lock. Now the man was helpless; if he didn't go wherever he was pushed, his arm would break.

"Forward, ever forward," said Rlllison firmly, "and don't try any more tricks."

"Don't go in there," the man screamed, "don't go in, you won't come out alive!"

Rollison stood quite still, with his prisoner still held in that unbreakable lock, only a foot or two from the door which he had been about to open. He felt a cold shiver running up and down his spine; it was a long time before he had felt as shaken as this. The fear in the man's voice was so shrill that he did not doubt that he told the truth; that at least he believed that if he went into the flat, he wouldn't come out alive.

Rollison asked, coldly: "Why?"

"There—there's a trap!"

"What kind of trap?"

"If—if you open the door wide——"

"Go on, or you'll really get hurt."

"If you open the door wide, it will—it will work like a flame gun!"

Rollison felt more coldness creeping along his spine, being quite sure that this was true.

"Who put it there?"

"We—we—we——"

"You and your gallant friend who ran out on you?"

"We had to!"

"I've heard that kind of I-didn't-mean-to-do-it story before," said Rollison, and eased his neck again. "Would you like to know something? I don't believe you." He started to push again, but as he did so the man back-heeled, and then tried to struggle, as if he would risk a broken arm or any other injury, would do anything at all to avoid going into that room.

"Well, well," said Rollison. "How is it rigged?"

"On—on—the wall above the door. There's—there's a release catch when the door opens."

"And it will fall down and explode, is that it?"

"Yes!"

"If that's the case, why did you come up the stairs when you expected me to open the door and be blown to bits?"

"We—we wondered what was up, whether you suspected——"

"Suspected what?"

"Whether—whether you suspected the trap. We wouldn't have come near enough to be hurt, the stairs would have saved us."

That was reasonable; and it coldly underlined his fear.

"Most interesting," observed Rollison. "I'll watch you burn under your own firecracker." He tightened his grip on the man's arm so much that the other could only stand there, a foot or two away from the door, his head twisted round so that he could stare at Rollison and beseech him.

"Don't make me go in there, don't make me go!"

Rollison said, softly: "Did the Doc send you?"

"Yes!"

"How did he know that I was after him."

"He—he—he—he——"

"I heard that part, and don't hold out because of what the Doc might do to you. If I don't get all the answers I shall push you into that room. I can, you know. How did he know?"

"He—he had a man watching Rickett, Rickett couldn't go anywhere without being followed, no one can. Rickett and his wife won't have a chance."

"I see. Where is Evie now?"

"I don't know!"

"What about Dan Rickett?"

"He—he's trying to get out of the country, I think; I don't know where he is now, I wasn't in the Guildford side of it, I just had my orders this morning."

"From the Doc?"

"Yes."

"Who *is* the Doc?"

Something seemed to happen to the big man. He moistened his lips and relaxed, no longer fighting against Rollison's pressure. There was something like derision in his voice when he answered:

"I don't know who the Doc is any more than you do! If

you think you've got a chance against him, you must be crazy."

"It takes people different ways," Rollison murmured. "So you don't know the Doc. How do you get his orders and how do you report?"

"I can tell you that, but it won't do you any good," the man said. "I use a broad who lives in Victoria, Lancing Hotel, Queen Street. But that won't help you——"

"What's her name?"

"Maggie."

"Maggie what?"

"Jeffson."

"I'll have to have a little talk with Maggie soon," promised Rollison, "she'll probably want to send some flowers to your funeral. Unless you prefer cremation. If you're really clever, you can push that door open an inch or two, and lift the firecracker off the wall. That way will be economical, and——"

All the man's fear came pouring back.

"No, don't try that," he begged, "don't try it, if it slips it'll do for us. I *know* it will. I've told you all I can, give me a break. D'you hear me? Give me a break."

"All right," said Rollison, quietly, "I'll give you a break." He released the man's hand, but brought the butt of the gun down just behind his ear; one blow was enough to make him fall, unconscious. It was a matter of seconds to rip off his tie, knot it about his ankles, then tie his wrists together behind him, using two handkerchiefs knotted together.

He pushed the man against the wall, then turned and hurried downstairs.

He stopped at the street door, but no one was waiting outside. He looked in both directions. The Bristol was where he had left it, but the black car had disappeared. He hurried out and along the street towards Gresham Mews, a little courtyard which had once housed the stables for the gentry in the terrace, and which now housed cars and one or two servants of the few remaining rich. An alley, leading from the mews led to the areas at the back of this side of Gresham Terrace, and led also to the fire escape at Number 22G.

No one was about.

Rollison climbed it, making the iron steps ring, and the handrail shake. A woman at a window half-way up stared at him in surprise; he waved to her. She did not come out on to the platform; probably she wasn't surprised at anything that her top flat neighbour did. He reached the back door of his own flat. It was locked and bolted, but long, long ago he had arranged a contraption beneath the fire escape platform, by which he could unbolt it from the outside. He heard the bolts slide back, unlocked the door, and pushed it open gradually. He found himself looking upwards, to see if any kind of booby trap was there.

He saw none.

He locked and bolted the door after him, then stepped into the small kitchen, which was spick and span and empty. He felt an easing tension as he went past the spare bedroom and his own, and then stepped into the living-room.

The first thing he saw had nothing to do with fire or booby traps.

His trophy wall had been stripped bare.

8

THE EMPTY WALL

WHERE there had been the hempen rope and the miniature gallows arm, the holed top hat, the cuckoo clock, the guns and knives, the poisons, the nylon stocking and the other trophies of the hunt, there was only the bare wall and a few fittings which looked bare and woebegone; as if the wall was aware that life had been stripped from it. In places the cream coloured wall-paper had faded. Here and there nails stuck out. The wooden back of a small box which had held three tubes of poison, used by a doctor who had killed three wives, had been broken. A litter of odd bits and pieces of fittings were on the floor.

That was all.

To Rollison, it was a kind of sacrilege, so stunning and unexpected that at first he could only stand and stare. Last night—*this very morning*—he had stood here and talked about so many of the trophies, touching them with the pride and fondness which one felt in old friends.

He said in a strangled voice: "One day I'll put his skull up there."

He kept staring. It was a great physical effort to move round, turning his back on the bare wall, and to go into the lounge hall. He saw the contraption which had been put just above the door, saw how delicately the trip-arm was poised—when the door opened a foot, it would push the arm, and——

What?

He took three long strides towards it as if, in his rage, he would wrench the booby trap down.

A yard away, he stopped abruptly.

He moistened his lips, and then moved much more slowly and cautiously, fetched a chair, and stood on it. Now he could look down on the booby trap. The incendiary shell was about the size of an egg, and was actually egg-shaped; the shell itself looked fragile. He didn't know what was in it, but felt quite sure that the man outside was right, and that if this fell and struck him, or the floor, it would explode. And it would spread fire and death; no man would have pretended to be so frightened as the man outside.

He lifted the 'egg' down, held it in the palm of his hand, and then stepped off the chair. At the last moment, the chair wobbled. He drew in a sharp hissing breath. The 'egg' rolled a little in his palm, but didn't fall; he kept his head, and did not grip it tightly. When he reached the floor, he was in a cold sweat again, and stood staring at the thing for fully ten seconds. Then he looked round, trying to decide the safest place to put it. There was nowhere in here. He went into the bedroom, took a pillow off his bed and tossed the pillow on top of the wardrobe, using his left hand for all this. Then he climbed up on another chair and deposited the 'egg' on the pillow. At least it wouldn't fall by accident, or topple over if anyone pushed the wardrobe.

He went back into the big room, glanced at the wall, and smoothed his forehead. When he opened the door, he was half prepared for trouble, and his hand was about the gun in his pocket, but there was only the man on the floor; wriggling. He was very close to the edge of the staircase.

Rollison pulled him in by the collar of his coat, dragged him across the hall and into the big room. Then he shut the front door, went back, undid the tie and pulled the man to his feet. He stood swaying.

"Did you take those things?"

"Ye-ye-yes."

"Doctor's orders?"

Gulp. "Yes."

"Passed on by Maggie?"

"Yes, I—Rollison——"

"Why take them if you were getting ready to burn the place down?"

"First—first we were told to take everything off the wall; it wasn't until afterwards that—that we had to lay the egg, we——" the man couldn't go on.

"How did you get the second order?"

"One of—one of the Doc's runners brought it; you—you don't seem to know a thing about the Doc."

"Tell me," Rollison invited.

He was feeling a little less tense; but very little. He hadn't slept for nearly thirty-two hours, and there had been the succession of shocks, none greater than the discovery of the old couple in their old world home. He was at a stage when he knew that unless he was very careful he would make some appalling mistake. He needed rest, and also time to think much more clearly—and he needed to know much, much more about the Doc. This man told him a little, mostly confirmation of what Grice had said, although with a few added items; for instance, that the Doc used runners who relayed messages which often came at third, fourth or fifth hand. The Doc had succeeded in covering his own trail so that he baffled not only the police, but the men who worked for him.

Rollison questioned the man for ten minutes, but learned little else. His name was Galloway, and letters in his pocket were addressed to J. Galloway, 51 Crane Street, Fulham. His driving licence had the same details. He knew his partner as Jack, but didn't know his surname, and he'd met him by appointment; certainly the Doc did not let anyone know too much.

Rollison took him into Jolly's bedroom, where there was a large wardrobe, made Galloway get inside and locked the door on him. It had been used as a temporary prison before, and there was no danger that the man would get out. He moved back into the big room, went across to the cocktail cabinet, and poured himself a stiff whisky-and-soda. As the soda was squirting, the telephone bell rang.

Grice?

He glared across, in no mood to talk to anyone; but there was no sense in that. He picked up the receiver, and barked:

"Rollison."

A girl said, in a startled way: "Eh?" He knew that it was Esmeralda, and the last thing he wanted was to exchange light badinage with her; but he had to be civil.

"This is Richard Rollison——"

"But Lothario," protested Esmeralda, "you sound as if you've failed to make a conquest for *months*."

"I don't forget you that easily," said Rollison, and for once he silenced Esmeralda. "Where are you speaking from?"

"Jane's house. I thought——"

"How's the baby?"

Esmeralda answered in a different, lighter tone, as if she was now talking about something which really mattered. The change was almost startling, and it brought Rollison his first moment's relaxation since he had reached Scotland Yard.

"Oh, he's *sweet*," said Esmeralda. "He's so tiny, it's hard to believe he'll grow up to be a—well, a grown-up. I haven't had much to do with babies, but if they're all like this I think I'll have to get better acquainted." She laughed as if she was coming out of a kind of trance. "Rolly, how did you sleep?"

"I didn't, I had to go out," said Rollison, "and I'm so tired now that I can hardly keep my eyes open."

"Poor, sweet Lothario," sympathized Esmeralda, "and I had to choose this minute to worry you. When do you think you will have had enough sleep?"

"Supposing I call you?"

"Do that," agreed Esmeralda, with surprising mildness, "but make a note of my flat telephone number; I've arranged to go back to Shepherd Market. It's Mayfair 91321." She paused while Rollison scribbled. "Got that?"

"Yes, thanks," said Rollison, "I'll call you some time to-night."

He heard her laugh as she rang off, and felt irritated, but that was as much with himself as with the girl.

He remembered what little he knew about her—partly from gossip, partly from what she had told him last night. She had thought herself likely to be wealthy all her life, but her parents had died leaving little money. Rather than sponge too much on her richer relatives, the Wylies, Esmeralda had modelled a little for reputable artists and photographers, had worked as a mannequin, had tried unsuccessfully to get on to the stage.

It was not exactly a unique story.

Nor was the tale of murder.

He could not get the sight of the old couple at Rose

Cottage out of his mind. Why had anyone, the Doc or any human being, thought it necessary to snuff out their lives as if it did not matter?

Who was the Doc?

Why had he talked of driving him, the Toff, out of the East End? Was it simply to avenge pretty Jessica Gay? How right was Grice in believing that there were people in the East End who believed that he, Rollison, had failed them? The East End seemed a long way off, but to Rollison it was as much the heart of London as was Mayfair. He felt a longing to go back there, to meet old friends by the dozen, to prove Grice wrong, to walk along the narrow, mean streets past the houses which had withstood the years and the bombing.

He made himself think of other things, and glared at the window, for no good reason, and tried to decide on the best thing to do next. Above everything else he wanted a reliable report from the East End on the Doc, and Ebbutt was the best source——

Why had Ebbutt been so cool?

"I'd better have forty winks," Rollison said. "If I tackle Maggie or anyone else in this shape, I'll make a hash of it."

At any other time he would have asked Ebbutt to send men to watch Maggie's hotel and Maggie herself, but Grice's talk of distrust was too vivid in his mind. He had to tell the police, or else let Maggie wait for an hour or two; and certainly he had to rest.

He went into his bedroom, glanced up at the top of the wardrobe, and suddenly wondered whether he could have been hoaxed. No; that man had shown genuine terror. He loosened his bow tie and collar, kicked off his shoes, and dropped on to the bed. Outside, the clear October sunlight showed that it was still no more than midday. Lying on his back, he telephoned Grice, not to say what had happened but to ask him whether the Wylies' home was being guarded yet.

"Yes, all laid on," Grice assured him.

"Fine," said Rollison. "Thanks. Now I'm going to have forty winks."

He rang off, telling himself that he could tell Grice more when Galloway had been in the wardrobe for a few hours; he might talk more freely, then, and so give Rollison more that he could tell Grice.

What else?

There was this 'Maggie'; his next job was to visit her. There was the baby, who should be quite safe now. There were the two fugitives from the Doc, Evie and Dan, who might now be his prisoners, and who might now be dead.

There were the trophies.

He had never realized how much they had meant to him. It had been easy to scoff at himself and the hobby of collecting, and at Jolly, his man, who had first disapproved of the trophy wall and finally become its curator. But now they were gone, almost certainly destroyed——

Had he any reason for thinking that?

There was no need to take them away to destroy them, that could have been done in the flat. So why had they been removed? He found himself wondering more about that, until it threatened to become an obsession. Then, with no warning at all, he dropped off to sleep.

While he was asleep, many people were thinking about him.

There was Esmeralda, sitting back in a taxi with a suitcase beside her, being taken from the Wylies' Mayfair home to her flat in Shepherd Market. She looked very *chic* and sweet; she sat with her knees close together and her hands folded demurely in her lap, and she watched the whirl of London traffic wide-eyed, as if she had never seen anything like it in her life; but there was another expression in her eyes, a kind of wicked mischief.

There was Jane Wylie.

She was in the spare room which had once been her own children's nursery, on the first floor of a large house in Mayfair, not ten minutes' walk away from Gresham

Terrace. The crib in which the baby slept was an old one. She stood looking down at the sleeping child, and her expression had the softness common to all women when looking at their own children, but to few when they are looking at the children of others. In the room were photographs of her own three boys and the family—John, twenty-seven when the first child had been born, forty-one when the last had been, forty-nine now. And there were her own pictures also showing the passing years.

There was Grice, talking to three C.I.D. men about the Rose Cottage murder; the Chief Constable of Surrey had called the Yard in.

There was a little, insignificant-looking man sitting in the corner of a third-class carriage on the way from Birmingham to London. He looked for all the world like a gentleman's gentleman, and that was not surprising, for that was what he was. He wore a black coat and striped trousers, and a bowler hat and furled umbrella were in the rack above his head. His once brown hair, grey now except for streaks here and there, was brushed as if lovingly across his high forehead, his face was lined and wrinkled, like that of an elderly man who had once been fat, and had lost weight. In losing weight, he appeared to have acquired a quality of sadness, which showed in his doleful, soulful brown eyes.

This was Jolly, who served the Toff, on his way to Gresham Terrace.

During the three hours while Rollison slept, all of these people thought a great deal about him. So did the Doc. So did men who served the Doc. So did Maggie, who had been warned that the Toff was likely to come to see her.

The child did not think at all, of course, but lay sleeping.

Jane Wylie, at three o'clock that afternoon, had a bridge party, and was out of the Throgmorton Square house, but among the staff was a children's nurse-turned-cook, who was probably even more capable than Wylie's wife.

It was the parlourmaid at the house who opened the door, just after three o'clock, to a good-looking young man who said that he had come to give the television its quarterly servicing. This was done regularly, and there were two television sets, one in the drawing-room on the first floor—across the landing from the nursery—and one in the servants' quarters.

"Better fix madame's set first," the maid said, "then you can come down to the kitchen and have a cup of tea while you're doing ours."

"Suits me fine," the young man said, "or it would do, if I had time." He grinned—and as the maid opened her mouth to scream, he dropped a cloth over her head and pulled it tight.

She tried to scream, but the sound was muffled.

Then, she struggled.

9

DOUBLE SNATCH

THE young man who claimed to have come to service the television felt the maid's body relax against his, then took the cloth away. The girl was a dead weight. He eased her from him, put an arm beneath her knees and another round her shoulders, and lifted her. Her head lolled back, and her red, ripe mouth was slack, showing her teeth. The man grinned, as if she could see him, and said lightly:

"You and I ought to get together sometime, sweetie."

He kicked open the door of the nursery, and carried the maid inside.

The child slept, without stirring, in the carved oak cot which had served the Wylies for so long.

The man carried the girl to an old rocking chair by the window, lowered her into it, and then took a cloth from his pocket and tied it round her mouth; next he took out cord, secured her wrists, then tied her legs to the chair. He did all this swiftly and expertly. Finished, he stood up, grinned at the girl again, and kicked the chair so that it started to rock to and fro, going back so far that it threatened to tip right over.

Then, he crossed to the cot.

He lifted the child out, without adjusting the blue shawl in which it was now wrapped. He went out. His big tool case was still on the landing, and he put the baby on the floor, and opened the case; it was empty. It was quite large enough for the child, and he put it in, tucked the shawl round, left the face uncovered, and closed the case. He examined the sides quickly, to make sure that none of the blue wool was showing, and then picked the case up by the handle, and started down the stairs.

Another servant, the cook who had once been a nanny here, was coming along the passage by the stairs, a woman in her forties.

"Hallo," said the young man, as he reached the hall. "I'm just nipping back to get one or two spare valves. More trouble than I expected."

"Oh, you're the television mechanic."

"That's me."

"Have you seen the maid who let you in?"

The young man grinned.

"Last time I saw her, she was singing rockaby baby or some such nonsense." He had an attractive smile, and the woman smiled back readily.

"Oh, the baby's all right then," the cook said; "I needn't go up."

"Suits me," the man said. "I won't be long."

"All right."

The cook opened the door, and the man stepped out, carrying the case quite casually. The door closed behind him, and he stepped towards the cars parked in Throgmorton Square—so close together that there wasn't room for another one, hardly room for a motor-cycle. He turned right, whistling just above his breath, and as he did so a tall man came towards him from one of the parked cars.

"Mind telling me where you're going?" he asked.

The man who was carrying the Rickett baby didn't turn to run, didn't turn a hair. He looked straight into the other's face, and asked:

"Mind telling me what business it is of yours?"

"This," the big man said, and took out a C.I.D. card. "What have you got in the case?"

"Tools."

"I'd like a look."

"Oh, well, I suppose I can't stop you," said the man with the case, and he actually grinned. He put the case down, close to the kerb, as if allowing plenty of room for passers-by. He did not appear to notice another heavily-built man coming up behind him—second plain-clothes detective, for Grice had put good men on to this job, and Ebbutt's men had gone.

The young man had trouble opening the case.

"Damn thing sticks," he grumbled. "I ought to have it seen to. Have to get a mechanic on the job!" He grinned again, and his manner was so carefree that neither of the Yard men seriously expected any trouble. Traffic was moving along the Square in one direction only, and a car was crawling up, as if the driver was hoping for a parking place.

The young man fumbling with the lock glanced up and saw the driver; another young man.

He winked.

The Yard men didn't notice that.

"Come on, get a move on," the first of them said, "or else let me have a try."

"Half a mo'," the young man said. "Ah, it's coming."

Then he straightened up, butting his head savagely into the speaker's stomach. The big man gave a groaning belch and staggered back. The other, by the youth's side, grabbed but couldn't hold him. The youth didn't try to get away but attacked him with both fists, smacking viciously into his face and stomach. As he did this, the driver of the car nipped out, grabbed the case and the child, and went back to the car. It was all done so swiftly and smoothly that no one noticed him, only noticed the two men who were fighting and the Yard man who had staggered back from the first impact.

The car roared off.

The Yard man tried to shout, but he was gasping for breath. Two passers-by stood watching the fight, others drew up. The youth tried to free himself now, but the Yard man grabbed his arm and he couldn't get away. He fought viciously and savagely, but suddenly crumpled up, as the Yard man smashed a fist into his stomach.

A uniformed policeman came, hurrying.

"Stop—that—car!" the Yard man gasped. "Dark blue—Austin Cambridge. Stop——"

By then, the car was out of the Square, and as soon as it turned the corner the driver pressed a button and both number plates changed.

Grice listened. . . .

"My God," he breathed.

Rollison heard the telephone bell, and took no notice. It didn't sound loud, but as if it was miles away. But it persisted. His head was heavy on the pillow, the last thing he wanted was to wake, but it wouldn't stop. He flickered his eyelids, and turned over, but still it went on—and then suddenly he was wide awake.

He picked up the telephone, and said: "Rollison speaking."

"Will you hold on a moment, sir? Mr. Grice would like to speak to you." The girl operator sounded cheerful.

"Oh, yes," Rollison said. "Thanks."

He waited, patiently at first. Grice was a long time—time enough to let him wish that he was asleep again. He most certainly had a headache. He started to frown, because Grice kept him so long, and then he heard a sound —*in* the flat. He caught his breath, and sat up very straight. The sound was repeated, and he had no doubt what it was: someone was turning a key in the lock of his front door.

He put the receiver down on the pillow, where it made no sound, and then pushed back the bedclothes. The door from the lounge hall opened; stealthily? Rollison picked up the gun which he had taken from his prisoner, hitched up his pyjama trousers, and approached the little passage leading to the kitchen, the living-room—the trophy room. Then came footsteps, and for the first time Rollison relaxed, and even grinned; for he could identify those footsteps anywhere in the world.

Jolly had come home.

Jolly would be a tower of strength; a second right arm.

Rollison went forward, to greet him. There was an extension telephone in the study, and he could take Grices' call from there. Grice was probably on the line now, wondering why there was no answer.

Jolly appeared, in the big room, as Rollison looked inside.

Jolly moved with a kind of restrained briskness, turned to close the door behind him, and then advanced into the living-room—and saw the bare, denuded wall. No man, pole-axed, could have been stopped more effectively. He stood with one foot slightly in front of the other, one hand raised, the other clenched by his side. The pose itself was quite a thing to see, but his face——

Rollison could see his reflection in a wall mirror.

He was horror-stricken.

Rollison, who knew him for a man who had schooled himself never to show emotion, had seen him in most moods, but never like this. Horror was the only word for his expression. He surveyed the wall from top to bottom and side to side, and then he closed his eyes, as if by doing that he could put away an evil vision. He opened his eyes again, and saw the truth that was inescapable; and he looked crushed.

"Not good, is it, Jolly," murmured Rollison.

Jolly started, and glanced round at him.

It was an odd moment, one which Rollison was often to think about in the future. For Jolly took a grip on himself with an obvious effort, squared shoulders which had drooped and a chin which had sagged, and advanced firmly.

"Good afternoon, sir," he said, "I'm very glad to see you again."

"And believe me, I'm glad to see you. You've landed in the middle of trouble, Jolly."

"So I perceive," Jolly said. He smoothed down his sparse hair and pressed his hand against his forehead, sure signs that he hadn't fully recovered. "Is there anything I can do for the moment, sir?"

"No. Get your things unpacked. Be careful of the man in your cupboard, I didn't tie him up, and I should think he will be annoyed. He's a big chap. Make it an inviolable rule never to bump against the wardrobe in my room, it might lay an egg you wouldn't like. If you've time, develop the film in the 35 millimetre camera, and see if a tyre print came out. I think Mr. Grice is on the telephone," added Rollison, and turned back to the bedroom after all; it was physically an ordeal to go into the study and stand near the bare wall.

"Very good, sir, and I won't be long," Jolly said.

No questions; no outburst of anger; nothing but the iron discipline of a man in ten thousand times ten thousand. Rollison found himself smiling as Jolly went into his own room, and then he hurried to the telephone and picked it up.

"Anyone still there?"

"Yes, sir, Mr. Grice still wants you," the bright-voiced girl said. "I'll put you through."

Grice was not always so patient, but Rollison gave that minor miracle little thought. He could hear Jolly moving about, and wondered what was really going on inside his man's mind. He felt better, and much less alone.

Then: "Rolly?" asked Grice.

Very slowly, Rollison said: "Yes, Bill," and waited. Thought of Jolly was wrenched away, everything was emptied from his mind except this call, for Grice's tone told a story of disaster which couldn't be mistaken.

"I'm damned sorry to have to tell you," Grice said, "but that baby has been taken from the Wylies' place."

Rollison didn't speak, just stood by the side of the bed, his face set as if it were a mask.

"I don't know how it was done yet, but there was some kind of a double snatch," Grice went on. "I called you as soon as I heard."

Now, Rollison spoke, stonily:

"How long ago?"

"Not more than fifteen minutes."

"Anything known?"

"The kidnapper was driving a dark blue Austin Cambridge."

"Thanks," said Rollison.

"Rolly——"

Rollison rang off, and turned to the wardrobe, opened it as if he had forgotten the 'egg' on top, took keys out of his hip pocket, knelt down and unlocked a drawer at the foot of the wardrobe. In here was a box, and inside the box two Webley automatics, each dull grey, and some clips of ammunition; there was also a thin bladed knife, without a sheath, but fastened to a large clip which could be fixed round his forearm or round the calf of his leg. He clipped the knife on to his right calf, slid one of the guns into his hip pocket, and a clip of ammunition in the left. Then he closed and locked the door. He glanced at himself in the mirror, and wasn't surprised to see the bleakness of his expression or the pallor of his face. He put on his collar and tie, and did up his shoes.

He went out.

"Jolly, I'm going to see a Miss or Mrs. Maggie Jeffson, at the Lancing Hotel, Queen Street, Victoria. If I'm not back in an hour, tell Grice."

Jolly appeared. "Very good, sir."

"No time to tell you what it's all about now, but in the middle of it there's a kidnapped baby and a cracksman named Rickett—Daniel Rickett. Get on to Bill Ebbutt, ask him what he knows about Rickett, and get Ebbutt's reaction to a character named the Doc."

"I think I know it now, sir," Jolly said. "While you were away——"

This wasn't the time to ask Jolly what he knew; but this would be testing time for Ebbutt.

"Well, check it. Tell Ebbutt I'll probably need a lot of help, and can he fix it."

"There is something I think you should know, sir," Jolly said in a tone which brooked no denial. "During your absence in New York, a number of Ebbutt's men turned against you, sir." Jolly's voice was now quite flat. "They believed you let them down badly by being away so long. Before you left, you said you would be back in a week or two."

"And instead it was nearly four months. Did anyone think of telling these gentlemen that for two months I was in hospital, and for six weeks, convalescing?"

"I tried to, sir," Jolly said, "but—well, the man known as the Doc was very active, sir, and you weren't at hand. The rumour spread that you were not ill or injured but—that the Doc had frightened you away."

"Well, they'll soon have a chance to see how scared I am," Rollison said. "All the same, tell Ebbutt what to do."

"Very good, sir," Jolly said.

Rollison went out, bleakly, telling himself that only one thing mattered.

That child was at the mercy of men who would kill without compunction, and there was just one lead that might take him to the child.

Maggie Jeffson.

10

MAGGIE JEFFSON

MAGGIE JEFFSON turned away from the telephone and moved to the window of her apartment in the Lancing Hotel. It was a small hotel, but luxurious; and the apartment had everything she could want.

So did she, if appearances told the truth.

She stood by the window, looking out into the street. If she raised her head, she could just see Birdcage Walk and part of the Mall, the deep autumn colouring of the plane trees lining the Mall, and the buildings in the distance, including the walls and roofs of St. James's Palace. She was young; probably in her early thirties. She wore a dark green dress with tiny golden spots on it, and with a neckline which must be nearly a record plunge. The astounding thing about her was her tiny waist, so unbelievably small that when men espied her for the first time, they usually gaped. Then, when they had studied her figure closely if surreptitiously, they wondered whether the small waist was real or illusory; whether it was not the magnificence of her bosom and hips which made the waist look small.

She had auburn hair, cut in loose curls, and the perfect complexion, except for a hint of freckles, which red-haired and green-eyed women often have.

An Austin saloon turned into the street from the direction of Birdcage Walk.

She turned swiftly, and went back to the telephone.

"Mary," she said when she was answered, "Mr. Brown will be here in a minute or two. As soon as he comes, send him straight up, and then arrange for the car to be driven to the garage, will you?"

"Yes, miss," Mary said.

Maggie Jeffson rang off, and turned back to the window.

Her movements were easy and natural, and had a natural voluptuousness that had to be seen to be believed. Had she been trying to attract the attention of a dozen millionaires, all competing for her favours, she could not have moved with greater seductiveness; and it wasn't put on, it was natural.

She stretched across a chair and took cigarettes from a small table, lit one, and let the smoke trickle out of her mouth. She had full lips, well-shaped but not excessively made-up; in fact she was hardly made-up at all.

Then, a telephone bell rang.

This was not one of the hotel extensions, but a line to the Westminster exchange. She moved across the lovely room, with its greens and golds, its velvets and brocades, and lifted the receiver from the cradle which matched the green of the table on which it stood.

"This is Maggie," she said.

A man asked, abruptly: "Heard from him yet?"

"He's on his way," she answered carefully.

"With it?"

"Yes."

"So they did it," the man said, and tension seemed to fade out of his voice. "I was beginning to wonder if Rollison lived under a lucky star. You know what to do next."

"I know," said Maggie.

"Don't let any harm come to it," the man said, and a new harshness sounded in his voice, "I don't want it dead, yet."

"I'll look after it," promised Maggie, "but what about——"

The man cut across her words.

"What about what?"

"We—we haven't heard from Galloway."

"We will," the man said. "Something went wrong at Rollison's flat, I haven't heard what, yet, but when I want you to worry, I'll tell you."

Maggie didn't smile. Her face had taken on a kind of impassiveness, and was very beautiful. With that slow, exciting walk, she crossed the room again, still drawing at the cigarette. The Austin was parked immediately outside the hotel, and she saw a man get into it and drive off. Before it was out of sight, the door bell of the apartment rang.

She went across and opened it.

"Hi, Maggie," a young man said, and came breezily into the room. "I've brought the prize packet. Ought to win a first in any show, I'd say." He waited until she had closed the door, and then lifted the case, swinging it a little, as if he were going to toss it into the air.

"Don't!" exclaimed Maggie.

"Now what's the matter with you?" asked the young man cheerfully. "I thought you had nerves of steel."

"He doesn't want—it hurt."

"So it better hadn't be," the young man said. "He's got enough bad news coming to him, as it is."

Maggie asked sharply:

"What's gone wrong?"

"The Toff oddity had a slice of luck," the other told her quietly. "His flat wasn't burned and he's still alive and kicking. He caught Galloway, too, and Galloway was good. The Doc won't be too happy about that when he knows."

"Why doesn't he know already?"

"Smith was with Galloway, and thought he was followed from Rollison's flat, so he went to earth until he knew he was safe."

Maggie's eyes, lacklustre until then, took on a kind of brightness.

"That's what *he* must have meant when he said he was beginning to think that Rollison had a lucky star." She watched the youth put the case down on a gold and green couch covered with a rich brocade, and saw him unfasten it. He pushed the lid back, and she took a step forward. "Is there anything else?" she asked.

"Penn was caught doing this job."

"*Penn*," she echoed.

"That's right. Two keymen gone in one morning," the

young man said, in a subdued voice, but his movements weren't subdued.

"Leo, be careful," Maggie said quickly, and moved forward.

He was taking the baby out of the case as if it was a bundle of rags; and actually held it upside down. She took it from him, and he made a grimace of distaste, watching her as she lifted the child to a level with her face, and looked at its screwed-up eyes and its little snub nose, the bubbles at its lips.

"It's okay, isn't it?" Leo asked abruptly.

"Yes, it takes a lot to harm a baby," Maggie said, slowly, and turned away from Leo, towards the bedroom. "I'm to keep it here until five o'clock, when he'll send for it."

"And we shan't know who he'll send or where it's going to be taken," Leo observed, and lit a cigarette as he followed her. He watched as she put the child gently down in an armchair, and hemmed it in with cushions. "If the Doc ever fires you, you could get a job as a children's nurse," he said; "you look as if you'd hate to see it hurt. I say, Maggie."

"What?"

"Ever get fed up with the Doc?"

She didn't answer.

"You know what I mean," said Leo, smoothly. "He takes us all for granted, doesn't he—and he doesn't really trust us an inch. Not a millimetre. We're watched and followed, all our movements traced, sometimes I think that if I want to pet a girl I'd have to ask his permission. I just wondered whether you ever felt like some of the others—that he's a bit too much of a good thing."

"You get your money, don't you?" Maggie asked.

"Oh, no complaints on that score. But can mere money buy loyalty, or will someone——"

"Leo," said Maggie Jeffson, "if I were you I'd get that nonsense right out of my head. I've worked with the Doc for much longer than you, and I've heard other people talk like you're talking now."

Leo looked at her levelly, appraisingly.

"And they're now daisy-pushing?"

"Yes."

"You have a point there," conceded Leo, grimacing. "But one of these days someone is going to put his nose out of joint. I feel in it my bones. Since Jessie was caught, he's been a hell of a sight worse than he was before; this man Rollison makes him see red. There's just one thing that would put the Doc in the hollow of one's hand, though."

"Is there?" Maggie asked.

"Just one. Knowing who he is. Do *you* know, Maggie?"

"No," she said, and it was impossible to be sure whether she was telling the truth, "and I don't think I'd try to find out. You're very young to die, Leo."

He stared at her.

He shivered.

"You really mean that, don't you?"

"I mean it."

"All right, I'll be good," said Leo, hastily. "I'll be very, very good." Then he moved swiftly and, taking her by surprise, gripped her wrists and held them very tightly. He was slim and supple and very strong, an inch or two taller than Maggie, and in a sharp-featured way, good-looking. He had a tight-lipped grin which didn't seem to reflect amusement as he drew her closer, so that she was squeezed tightly against him.

"Maggie," he breathed, "you wouldn't tell him that I had this little *tête-à-tête* with you, would you? Because if you did I would in turn tell him a thing or two—not all of them true, perhaps, but with plenty to suggest that perhaps you'd worked with him *too* long. He expects loyalty but he doesn't give it much, does he? If he suspected you were——"

"I won't tell him what a fool you are," Maggie said. She didn't try to free herself, but stood limp and relaxed, as if a door were pressing against her, not a lean, lithe youth.

Leo laughed.

"Do you want to know something?" he said, lightly. "You and I could go places."

Then, from the next room, from a man who was out of sight, there came a mild chuckle and a gentle question.

"*Could you, Leo? Then why don't you?*"

Leo swung round, and Maggie stared towards the door, unbelieving. No one was in sight, but the echo of that voice seemed to be in their ears, with its hint of mocking laughter.

"*Could you, Leo? Then why don't you?*"

They kept absolutely still. Nothing moved, once the voice had stopped, it was almost as if the words had come out of the air, and had floated away through the open window. The sound of traffic came in, muted and faraway.

Leo said, abruptly: "Who was——" and then broke off. He put his right hand to his pocket, and drew out a gun; one exactly like that which Rollison had taken from Galloway. "You stay here," he said, and moved swiftly towards the door. He didn't go into the big room, but stood close to the door, and sidled nearer.

The unseen man spoke again.

"You don't really think that gun will help you, Leo, do you?" he said.

Leo didn't answer.

Maggie Jeffson turned and looked at the sleeping child, then almost wildly at the window. She didn't pick the child up, but moved to the other side of the bed; here was another telephone, an extension of the one with the direct line. She picked it up, and dialled.

"Calling for help?" inquired the unseen man lightly. "Oh, well, fair's fair, you fetch the Doc and I'll fetch the cops. I suppose it had to happen sooner or later. Unless, of course, you care to tell the Doc that the Toff doesn't like the cops and will make it a free-for-all just between our two selves. Nothing barred except babies. If he wins, he can keep my trophies of the hunt, if he loses he wills me his ribs to place high upon the wall."

Leo was crouching, and creeping towards the door, the gun thrust forward.

"Can you hear me, Maggie?" called Rollison, in a brighter tone than ever.

She was listening to the ringing sound of the telephone, her body rigid, her eyes frightened as she stared towards the door. There was silence as she watched Leo, who was now so close to the door that he couldn't get any nearer without being seen. His face was set and his eyes blazing, and his finger seemed to be quivering on the trigger.

"Mind you don't get in a draught," called Rollison, solicitously, "you won't be much use to the Doc wid a code in de dose."

There was no sound in the room, and after Rollison stopped speaking, the only thing that Maggie could hear was the *brrr-brrr-brrr* of the ringing sound; but the Doc did not answer and no one answered for him.

"I'll tell you what," said Rollison, "I'll make a deal. If you come into this room bringing the baby with you, Maggie, I'll just take you and the baby, and beat it. I won't tell the police where I found the precious infant, I'll just let it be a warning to the Doc. He'll be intrigued to find out whether I can make Maggie talk, too. Yes?"

Leo had moved a few inches from the wall. He was going to spring forward, fling himself into the big room, and shoot Rollison. His lips were parted, and his teeth showed; he had an ugly, savage look.

"No, I perceive," went on Rollison, as if sorrowfully. "I was afraid not. I'd better bring the police——"

Then, Leo spoke.

"If you call the police, I'll cut the kid's throat," he said, and sounded as if he meant it.

Maggie stood stock still, looking down at the child, listening to that unending *brrr-brrr-brrr*. After Leo's threat there was no sound and no movement from the other room; it was almost as if Rollison had vanished into thin air.

Then, the ringing sound stopped, and a man said in a

deep voice which was almost as familiar to Maggie as her own:

"Who is that?"

"Rollison's here with me," Maggie whispered, very softly, "he's in the other room, Leo and I are in the bedroom. He wants the baby."

The Doc did not even seem to pause to think.

"Hold him there," he ordered. "Never mind how, but hold him there, I've had enough of Mr. Ruddy Toff, I'll send someone to put him where he belongs."

Then he rang off.

11

BARGAINING

ROLLISON stood near the door of the big room of the apartment, with the passage door closed behind him. He had not moved from the time he had come in. He could see all of the big room, and the open door of the bedroom—and there was something else he could see, although the others did not yet realize it. Leo was plainly visible in a long dressing-table mirror, and by standing close to the edge of the door, Rollison could see without his own reflection showing. The woman wasn't, nor was the child; but the foot of the bed, the door, and the crouching man were right in Rollison's line of vision.

He had heard the faint whirring of the telephone, and knew that the woman must have dialled a number; and then for a long time there had been no sound from her until, suddenly, she had started to whisper. Soon, the help she had summoned would be on the way.

Above all, Rollison wanted the child; unhurt. After that,

he wanted a line to the Doc, and had hoped to find it here. But he wouldn't, now. He had given up the advantage of surprise, hoping to startle and to bluff these two into a mistake, but Leo wasn't going to be bluffed.

Rollison saw Leo stand up as he made the threat to kill the child—and then Leo did something which made the threat seem positively devilish. He took a knife from his pocket. His expression, nearly full face in the mirror, had brutal viciousness, and he looked as if he would carry out his threat gladly. Obviously he now knew that he could be seen in the mirror. He began to back towards the head of the bed, and if he went much further he would be out of Rollison's sight.

"Leo," Rollison said, "don't move any more."

The youth stopped.

"I've told you what I'll do," he spat out. "I——"

"Leo," Maggie Jeffson said in a steady voice, "don't lose your head. *He* said that we mustn't harm the baby."

"That's what he told you," sneered Leo; "he told me to suffocate it if I couldn't get it away alive."

The Doc was quite capable of ordering that.

Maggie didn't answer, and that seemed to imply that she believed Leo. Leo moved again, until all Rollison could see was his back. He heard a sibilant sound, as of whispering; they were talking to each other so that he couldn't hear. He knew that Leo had that gun and felt quite sure that he would use it.

It was more than half an hour since Rollison had left Gresham Terrace, and Jolly would wait for sixty minutes exactly, not a split second more, before calling Grice and naming the hotel. So it would be forty minutes, say, before the police arrived.

To reach the telephone he must pass the bedroom door, and make himself an easy target.

But the woman had sent for that help; he probably hadn't more than ten minutes' grace—if as much.

The whispering stopped; then the woman spoke quietly. She had a pleasant voice, very different from Evie Rickett's, different from Esmeralda's, too, for it had a huskiness and richness. Rollison had not yet set eyes on her, but her voice gave him some idea of what to expect.

"Mr. Rollison," she said, "you've been away from London for a long time, you don't quite know what's happening. You're making a mistake in fighting the Doc."

"Mistake for whom?" asked Rollison interestedly. "The Doc or for me?"

"I'm quite serious," she went on. "Before you left England he was hardly known, but to-day—well, you're making the biggest mistake of your life."

"What would you like me to do?" asked Rollison curiously. "Bow out and wish him luck?"

She hesitated.

"Not quite that?" murmured Rollison. "Nice of you."

"There is one thing you could do," said Maggie Jeffson, and a new tone in her voice told Rollison that she was anxious to make him think she was really serious, that this was the crux of what she had to say. It was probably the result of the whispering campaign between her and Leo. "You could work *with* the Doc."

"Oh, no," ejaculated Rollison. "Not that old trick."

"You'd be wise, and if you don't you'll regret it, because —well, a lot of people will get hurt. That's one thing that even the police don't realize yet, the Doc always gets what he wants."

"Even dictators die."

"If I can't make you see reason now," Maggie said patiently, "but why won't you think about it—that wouldn't do any harm, anyhow. You can't take the baby back, Leo would rather do what the Doc told him. You don't want the baby to die, do you?"

Leo said smoothly: "I'd kill it all right."

"So why don't you give up trying," insisted Maggie, "why don't you consider working for the Doc?"

Rollison didn't answer.

"Just think what a combination it would be," Maggie went on, and there was a note of excitement in her voice.

"Between you, you could do everything you want. The Doc always said that you had the strongest potential in the East End, that he'd always prefer to work against the police than you; he could guess what the police were going to do next, but you might fool him. I'm *quite* sure that he'd like to work with you."

"Well, well," said Rollison, as if bemused, and added: "Well."

"*I'm* not so sure," Leo said roughly.

"If you like," offered Maggie, "I'll telephone the Doc now."

She was just playing for time; nothing else at all.

Rollison turned, and locked the door which led from the passage, then shot the bolt at the top, sliding it slowly and with no sound. As far as he could see, there was no other way into the flat except by the window. He hadn't spoken for a long time. He heard Leo mutter, and wondered how long the man's patience would last.

"There isn't a thing that you and Doc couldn't do if you worked together," Maggie said, with soft insistence.

"I can believe it," said Rollison.

He moved forward in long, silent strides, picking up a chair as he went. He knew the exact position of the mirror and of the couple, and believed that he couldn't be seen now. He stood squarely in front of the bedroom door, so that he could see the head of the bed, the dressing-table and the wardrobe; the man and the woman and the baby must be in the far corner, keeping out of his sight in the mirror.

He flung the chair.

He heard Maggie exclaim and Leo swear, then he followed the chair, in a wild surge forward. He saw the woman, crouching over the armchair, and guessed that the baby was on it. He saw Leo, gun in hand, bringing it up to firing position; the hurtling chair had taken him off his guard, but not for long. Rollison dived on to the springy bed and then rolled over. He felt a bullet tug at his trouser leg as he struck out, hit Leo and sent him staggering. He had only seconds to work. Leo was still staggering as Rollison reached his feet, grabbed the youth by the neck, and thrust him away. Leo's arms were waving, the gun pointing towards the ceiling, but in a moment he would level it; and in that moment——

Rollison cracked the youth's head against the wall

Leo's eyes rolled, and his knees bent under him.

Rollison saw the youth falling, and saw Maggie moving. He turned round to face her. His hair was dishevelled and his coat rucked up, but he looked so bland, so nonchalant and so recklessly handsome that she probably didn't notice anything else.

"Hallo, Maggie," he said cheerfully, "nice to know you. You haven't let that child come to any harm, have you?" He moved closer to her, but she didn't back away, just stood over the chair as if she, not he, was guarding the child. The telephone was on a shelf built into the wall, and he stretched out for it, lifted the receiver and tucked it under his chin, and then dialled so that he had one hand free. He saw the eagle way she watched, and as he called his own Mayfair number, he said in deep and convincing tones: "Whitehall 1–2–1–2." He flashed her a smile. "That's the number of Scotland Yard, or did you know?"

She just stared at him.

It wasn't a moment to pay much attention to a woman's looks or figure, but Rollison's gaze roamed about her, and what he saw seemed to please him, too.

Then, Jolly answered.

"Hallo, Jolly," he said, "I think I'm all right, so don't tell Grice anything about this place just yet."

The woman drew a deep breath.

"But I need help of a kind," Rollison went on. "I fancy that in ten minutes or so some of the doctor's orderlies will be coming to pay their respects, and I'm not sure that I want to be alone when they come. Did you talk to our pal?"

"As a matter of fact, sir, I did," said Jolly, "and Ebbutt said that he was very anxious to see you. He promised assistance though, and he is on the way now—I expect him almost any minute. I took the precaution of suggesting that it would not be wise for him to come alone."

"Good. Send them straight over here, Jolly. Apartment 101, on the fifth floor. Tell them they might run into a lot of trouble, and they'd better be careful—make sure he knows I'm having Doc trouble, too."

"I will, sir," Jolly said, and then his voice rose slightly: "There is a ring at the door now, sir—two long one short, that will *be* Ebbutt."

"Tell him not to lose any time," Rollison urged.

He rang off, on Jolly's calm assurance, and he looked into Maggie Jeffson's beautiful eyes. She seemed completely untroubled, but it was a forced composure; she was skilled in hiding her feelings.

"When the Doc's friends come," Rollison said earnestly, "tell them to go away in a hurry or I shall send for the police. Tell them to let the Doc know that I'm holding you as a hostage, and that he'll be hearing from you soon. And tell them not to lose any time."

Unexpectedly, her lips curved at the corners; there was a smile in her eyes, too. Was she laughing at him? She lifted the gilded telephone and must have been answered by the operator on the instant.

"Mary . . ." she began.

"I'm expecting two or three friends," she went on. "Have they arrived yet?

"Oh. Well, when they come, tell them to go back and report that I've had to change arrangements, and I'll be getting in touch with them again later. Then let me know what they say. . . .

"Thank you, Mary."

She rang off, putting the receiver down slowly. That seemed almost like a signal, for Leo to stir on the floor, and for the baby to give a weak, bubbly cry. Rollison glanced towards it, saw the dark blue eyes wide open, the pink-and-red face puckered, the lips turned back to show the bare red gums.

"Will they do what you tell them?" Rollison asked.

"I think so."

"You'd better hope so, too. How bad a man is Leo?"

"Pretty bad," she said, quietly.

"Too bad to let loose."

She was still smiling, but obviously puzzled now. She glanced, as if without thinking, at a photograph standing on a small table—a photograph of a dark-haired, good-looking man, and when Rollison saw it, his eyes narrowed.

He had seen a similar portrait, of the same man—in Esmeralda Gale's handbag; she had taken it out when looking for her lipstick at the Star Club.

Until that moment, he had not dreamed of a possible association between this woman and Esmeralda.

Could there be?

Maggie Jeffson looked at Leo, who was trying to sit up, but who had not yet recovered consciousness completely; his was more a reflex movement at the moment. Rollison and the woman studied each other, while there were the sounds of traffic from outside, and then, very clearly, a car racing along the street and stopping too sharply; its brakes squealed.

"The Doc's orderlies," murmured Rollison.

She said: "Probably."

"Now we'll see how much notice they'll take of you," said Rollison. He grinned and looked completely at ease; but he was not. A locked and bolted door would not keep determined men out if they had orders to get in and kill. He could call the police and save himself, but that wasn't what he wanted to do yet. There were other ways of fighting the Doc. He moved swiftly, to push two heavy chairs against the door, as a kind of barricade.

Would those killers do what Maggie expected?

She looked like a statue of Juno in modern dress as she waited, revealing a most remarkable trick of immobility. Rollison saw the look of repose come back, so that her face seemed like delicately tinted marble, but she was as much on edge as he. He didn't know whether she expected the men to obey her, or whether she had known all the time the they would not.

He would soon know.

The telephone bell rang, startling Maggie, although she must have been expecting it. She hesitated, then lifted the receiver and said:

"Yes?"

Rollison stretched out a hand and took the instrument from her, and listened as the girl Mary said in a breathless voice:

"They wouldn't take any notice, Miss Jeffson. They're on their way up now."

12

MAN ALONE

ROLLISON put the receiver down slowly. He did not need to tell Maggie what had happened; obviously she guessed. He tried to judge her real reaction, but couldn't be sure of it; all expression had gone again, her eyes were lack-lustre, her lips seemed to be set more tightly. He saw her glance down at the child, who had become quiet again, but at that very moment it opened its mouth and cried weakly:

"*Ya-ah-ya-ah-ya.*"

There was no sound from the passage, yet.

Rollison said quietly: "You'd better go and reason with them, Maggie. Tell them that if they break the door down, they'll get me only over your dead body." He gave a mechanical smile, and moved aside for her to pass—and as he did so, the telephone bell rang again.

Maggie swung round. It was hard to believe that a human being could move so beautifully, that a human body could call so loudly to a man.

"What——" she began.

Rollison lifted the receiver, trying to keep his mind empty of guessing. If Ebbutt's men weren't too long, those chairs would hold. He couldn't get heavier furniture out of the rooms and into the passage to strengthen the barricade; he had done all he could.

"Hallo?" he said abruptly.

"Mr. Rollison," said Jolly, and his voice had a different note, one almost of anguish. This caused more alarm than anything else. "I've been talking with Mr. Ebbutt, and he flatly refuses to come. I told him that it might be a matter of life and death to you, and he still refuses. I will come the moment——"

He broke off.

There was a noise at the other end of the line, and then a different voice, deep, hoarse, powerful. There was only one voice exactly like that in the world; the voice of Bill Ebbutt, ex-prizefighter, friend and stalwart and supporter of the Toff for as many years as Rollison liked to recall, a man who had been loyal when everyone else had failed, when the police had hunted and even bosom friends had denied the Toff's name.

"Mr. Ar," Ebbutt said, and seemed almost to be pleading. "I'd come like a shot if this was a n'ordinary job, you know that, but I can't fight the *Doc.* I just can't, Mr. Ar, 'e's told me that if I do 'e'll cut me gran'child's froat."

Ebbutt stopped.

And into the harrowing silence there came the thud of footsteps in the passage outside.

The footsteps drew nearer.

Maggie, staring at Rollison, began to move away as if she was going to plead with the men; or else, to push away the chairs and unbolt the door, and so make it easier for them. At least Rollison could make sure that she could be stopped from doing that.

"Honest, Mr. Ar, if it was anyfink else——"

"All right, Bill," said Rollison, quietly, "I see the point."

"*Will you give me that telephone?*" Jolly cried in a shrill voice, "*I want to call Scotland Yard.*"

Rollison rang off.

Maggie had gone out of the bedroom, now. Rollison moved quickly, picked up the photograph of the man whom Esmeralda knew, and slipped it out of its frame and into his pocket. He picked up the baby, and followed the woman. A man was working at the lock of the door; he hadn't troubled to press the bell, and was obviously just prepared to get the door open and burst in. There might be two or three men there.

Or—one might be preparing to throw an 'egg'.

That was the greatest danger. If they opened the door and flung the 'egg' inside they could burn the apartment to nothing, but be in no danger themselves.

Maggie looked round at him.

"I don't think they'll listen to me," she said flatly. "I can try, but I think it will be a waste of time."

"All right, Maggie," Rollison said, in the same level tone of voice that he had used when speaking to Bill Ebbutt. "Do you know what they'll do?"

"They'll probably set fire to the place."

"Knowing you're here?"

"I told you before," the woman said, "you haven't even begun to know the Doc. If you work for him, this is a risk you take."

"So it's a risk you take," Rollison said, and found himself smiling almost bitterly. "He might at least give you evens." He turned away from the passage door, as the handle turned; only the bolt held it now, undoubtedly the lock had been picked. He closed the door of the big room, held the baby in one arm, and held Maggie's wrist with the other. He went to the window, and said:

"Open it as wide as you can."

"But——"

"Open it."

She hesitated for a moment, then flung the window up. Cold air swept into the room, making the curtains billow, ruffling the blue shawl and making the fluffy wool dance like blue corn in a late summer breeze. Rollison took out his lighter and held it to one of the cushions on the couch near the window, waited until it was flaming and smouldering, and watched the dark smoke drawn out of the window. He leaned out, and shouted:

"*Fire! Send for the fire service. Fire!*"

He saw startled people look up. The smoke was passing over his head, something in the cushion was burning with a most offensive smell. He saw a woman point upwards, and a policeman come running from the corner.

"Fire!" Rollison bellowed. "Fire! We can't get out, the passage is blazing. *Fire, fire, fire!*"

The policeman was waving, as if to reassure him, while a man dashed into a nearby shop. To telephone? Rollison drew back, still holding the child. Maggie, in the same statuesque pose, was standing near the window and watching him as if she had never seen anything like him before.

Then there was a roaring noise from the passage; a crash, as if the door had been forced down. Rollison drew his gun from his pocket, and covered this door—but he did not need a gun and he did not need telling what had happened.

The roaring was of burning.

The 'egg' had burst, the outer door was down, the fire was a fire in deadly earnest, and the only question was how long it would take to spread in here.

Then, he *knew*.

He could see the inside of the door blackening already, and the flames ate into it voraciously; in a matter of minutes, every part of the apartment would be afire.

"When you're up against the Doc," said Maggie Jeffson, "you just can't win."

The sound of a fire engine came loud and clear and urgent, and people were running towards the corner, to see it, while crowds gathered outside the Lancing Hotel. Men were hurrying away from the entrance—probably these were the Doc's men, who had started this thing.

Rollison leaned out of the window, waving both arms.

"The place won't last five minutes!" he roared. "Get everyone out! Everyone out!"

He couldn't be sure whether the policeman heard, but he saw men turn towards the officer and guessed that they were passing on his message. He heard the fierce crackling of the flames outside the room, and an explosive *zutt* as a panel of the door cracked.

Flame leapt through it, blasting hot.

The fire engine turned the corner.

Rollison saw it pull up outside the hotel, and saw steel helmeted men leap from it and start to uncoil the hoses. The fire escape arrived and the ladder and platform seemed to shoot up towards him. He knew that he was safe and that for the time being he had saved the child. No matter how fierce the flames nor how hot they seemed, they would escape.

Smoke was writhing towards him, thick and evil-smelling, when the fireman arrived atop the turntable.

"Take the baby and help her," Rollison said, and he seemed almost detached as the fireman took the child, then steadied Maggie. "And there's an unconscious man inside."

"We'll see to him," a man said.

"I'm all right," Maggie said, evenly. She gave Rollison that unexpected, half amused smile, then stepped on to the turntable. The roaring from behind was steady and almost deafening, now, and Leo wasn't likely to live through it, in spite of the fireman's words.

Then, Maggie staggered.

The fireman was still holding her with one hand, the infant hugged closely to him with the other. Maggie closed her eyes, and swayed backwards. Rollison stretched out and tried to grab her, clutched her dress, and felt it tear in his grasp. The fireman held on desperately, but her dead weight pulled him towards the edge, and with the child in his arms he might lose his balance.

He let go.

Then Maggie Jeffson fell.

There came a scream from below, rising as if in awful terror—then silence, next a thud, then a crowd of horrified people about the crushed body on the pavement.

Rollison stared down, hard-eyed.

"Get a move on, or the place'll be up like a perishing Guy Fawkes," the fireman burst out. He was pale, and was obviously keeping his face averted from the ground and from the woman. "What the hell made her do that? If she'd kept her head for another couple of minutes, we'd have been okay."

The fire roared behind them and tongues of flame leapt out. Leo was lost in the flames, was almost certainly dead by now.

Rollison climbed on to the swaying platform.

Among the men who were on the opposite side of the road, ten minutes later, was Superintendent Grice. There were dozens of police, and more were coming on duty every moment. Three fire engines were pumping water on to adjoining buildings, for it was obvious that there was no hope at all of saving any part of the Lancing Hotel. Rope barricades had been put up at the corner, and the crowd was being thrust slowly back. An ambulance stood by, and the body of Maggie Jeffson was being covered with a white sheet.

An ambulance man held the baby.

By then Rollison had recovered from the overpowering heat upstairs, and was standing near Grice, watching the stretcher bearers and drinking a cup of hot, sweet coffee which had been brought by a café owner round the corner.

Grice called sharply: "Stop a minute."

He went towards the dead woman, and bent down. A young doctor who had formally pronounced that life was extinct, drew near him.

Rollison watched.

Grice pushed the magnificent auburn hair back from the marble forehead, then let it fall again. He spoke in an undertone to the doctor, then signalled to the ambulance men to carry on. It wasn't until the doors had closed on what was left of the Doc's loyal servant, that Grice made his way to Rollison.

Grice looked a different man; older, graver, harassed.

"Did you see what I was looking for?" His manner was abrupt.

"I think so. A bullet hole."

"Did you know?"

"I knew she didn't faint and I knew she didn't throw herself off," Rollison said, "but I don't know who fired at her. Someone from a window opposite, of course. Possibly they were after me—she moved in front of me just before she started to fall."

"The cold-blooded swine," Grice said, and his voice was harsher than Rollison could ever remember. "I knew the Doc was as bad as they come, I knew he was squeezing the East End, I knew he was squeezing out the other fences and setting himself up as a kind of Big Boss, but I thought we could afford to wait for a while. I didn't think he'd——"

Grice broke off.

He hadn't dreamed, and no one had dreamed, that the Doc would go to lengths like these; that if he were thwarted he would use fire to kill and to maim the innocent, if only he could get his own revenge.

"I'll have the building opposite searched," Grice said, "but I'll bet it's far too late."

He gave orders, and then a Fire Service officer came up, tall, black-haired, glum.

"Can't be sure yet, but it looks as if two families were trapped," he said. "We've talked to one of the porters and to someone on the third floor. Can't find anyone else, there wasn't a big staff."

Rollison said quickly: "Have you found the telephone operator? A girl named Mary?"

"No, sir. The porter *thinks* she went up to the fourth floor to warn a deaf woman who couldn't hear the telephone," the fire officer said. "Can't be sure."

"I'm sure of one thing," Grice said. "I won't rest and the Yard won't rest until we've got the swine." He looked bleakly into Rollison's eyes. "I know you saved the child, perhaps we wouldn't have if you'd told us where to come. But if you'd told us, we might have stopped this holocaust."

Rollison didn't speak.

"Why didn't you call us?" Grice demanded, roughly. "What makes you think you're so all-powerful?"

Rollison rubbed his chin where it was sore from banging it on a rung of the fire escape. He did not smile and did not relax as he said evenly:

"I asked you to guard the baby. A nice job you made of it. If you're handing out blame, get in line yourself."

He turned and pushed his way through a crowd of firemen, policemen and newspapermen. Two newspapermen recognized him and came hurrying, but he wouldn't stop, and the look in his eyes and the set of his chin told them that he wasn't just being difficult. A police sergeant sent an inquiring glance at Grice, asking silently if Rollison was to be stopped; Grice shook his head. Rollison pushed his way towards the corner of the street which led to Birdcage Walk. There was a big crowd here, too, but clear above the hum of talk he heard his own name.

"Mr. Rollison! This way, Mr. Rollison!"

That was Jolly.

Rollison looked across the road and saw Jolly standing by a taxi; bless Jolly, now and always. Rollison skipped between the traffic, most of which was moving very slowly, and climbed into the taxi. Jolly got in beside him, gave the driver the address, and then sat back, his body upright, while Rollison leaned in a corner and closed his eyes, as if he wanted to shut out the picture of ugly things.

Jolly sat without saying a word.

As they turned into the Mall, heading for Clarence

House and then St. James' Street, Rollison opened his eyes.

"Nice welcome home for you, Jolly."

"That is hardly a matter of concern, sir."

"No. Ebbutt gone?"

"Yes, sir, and obviously he was acutely distressed. There appears to be no doubt at all that this man who is known as the—ah—the *Doc* has succeeded in dominating Ebbutt and many others, usually by threatening members of their family. As appears to be the case in this instance, sir. The most disquieting thing is that I do not think we will be able to call upon Ebbutt for any information or any active assistance of any kind. In fact, I think it at least conceivable that Ebbutt will ask *you* not to continue with the campaign, in case the—ah—Doc stages a kind of reprisal war among those known to be or to have been sympathetic towards you. Ebbutt didn't exactly put it in that phraseology——"

"He wouldn't," said the Toff, and smiled wryly. "Anyhow, *you* don't change. Make that a rule, Jolly. Is the wardrobe in your room still locked?"

"Firmly, sir."

"That's something, although it probably isn't much," said Rollison. "Well, we won't be long." The car turned out of Piccadilly and the second on the left would be Gresham Terrace. "I think you'd better nip back and get the car, Jolly; you can take this cab."

"I doubt if that will serve any purpose, sir," Jolly objected reasonably. "The car was parked with several others near the hotel, and I think it was badly damaged. I'll check if you wish, sir, but——"

They turned the corner.

Rollison didn't answer, and Jolly saw his expression change into one that was near bewilderment. A black Rolls-Bentley was parked outside 22 Gresham Terrace, and Sir John Wylie and his wife were coming away from the house; obviously they had given up hope of finding anyone in.

The Wylies stood and waited as the taxi drew up; and Rollison saw the despair on Jane Wylie's strong, handsome face.

13

JOLLY IN FORM

"You make yourself invisible and hurry upstairs," Rollison said to Jolly. "Let's try to make things seem as normal as we can."

"Very good, sir."

"Right," said Rollison, and pressed his hand against his forehead. The tension at the Lancing Hotel, the choking smoke, and the shock of seeing Maggie Jeffson die, had done little to clear his mind. He saw Jolly look at him with evident concern, but took no notice. The cab drew up outside the house, and Jane Wylie exclaimed:

"There he is!"

"And here I am," said Rollison, forcing his black mood away. He opened the door while the cab was still moving, and jumped out. "Hallo," he greeted. "Just in time."

They looked as if they were shaken by the sight of him. He didn't know that his hair had been singed, that his face was blackened with smuts, that his coat was torn and that his eyes held what seemed to be a kind of feverish brightness. At least, their surprise gave him a momentary ascendancy. He took Jane Wylie's hand and dug a smile out of the depth of his resilience, and said:

"We've got the baby back, unhurt."

Wylie cried: "You have?" and looked delighted beyond words. "Jane—Jane, my dear, it's all right, the child's *safe*." In his eager reassurance, he was as nearly emotional as Rollison would ever expect him to be. He took his wife's arm and held her tightly, while she looked into Rollison's face, her eyes clearing of some of their distress.

"Is that—is that really true?"

"The police are in charge of him now."

"Yes. If you'd gone to the police in the first place——" Wylie broke off.

"I know," said Rollison, quietly. "Believe it or not, I did go. Two Yard men were outside your house at the time of the kidnapping. I don't know exactly what happened then, but at least all's well again now."

"Thank goodness for that," Wylie said, and then began to mumble and speak in odd phrases again. "Foolish, of course—Jane blamed herself. Bridge party, y'know, and——"

"I don't think I'll ever want to play bridge again," said Jane Wylie. "When I heard——"

"You probably wouldn't have been able to stop it," Rollison said, "don't start blaming yourself, enough people are doing that already. I heard something about a maid being attacked. Was she badly hurt?"

"Frightened, mostly," Wylie said, and coughed. "Naturally."

"Is there anything else we can do?" Jane asked, and she freed herself from Wylie's grasp and put a hand on Rollison's. "You look dreadful, you ought to go and get some rest. But what on earth happened?" There was intentness as well as bewilderment in her expression. "Why should anyone want—whose *is* this baby?"

"He's the child of a couple named Rickett, who seemed to think he was safer with me than with them," Rollison said quietly. "They're running away from trouble in the East End."

"So it isn't——" Jane Wylie began, and stopped abruptly.

"Tell me, Rollison." Wylie cut across his wife's words, and so stopped the 'yours' which had so nearly come. He looked mildly embarrassed, and coughed again. "Anything we can do to help? No? Well, be advised—Jane's quite right. You must rest. Sure there's nothing we can do?"

"There might be, later."

"Call on me," said Wylie, and then corrected himself as he took his wife's arm. "Us. Good-bye for now."

Rollison stood and watched them go.

Jolly had paid off the taxi, and was waiting in the flat. Rollison found his feet dragging a little as he went upstairs. The door was ajar. He closed it as he stepped inside, and looked round; nothing had changed in the lounge hall, but there was a significant change in the study. The nails had been taken out of the wall, the odd pieces of case fittings were gone, and the wall was clear and clean. Jolly was in the kitchen, and cutlery was clattering.

Rollison went after him.

Jolly spoke without turning round, for he was at the oven, wearing an apron, and looking so endearingly normal that it was hard to believe that they were in the midst of disaster.

"If you will allow me to make a suggestion, sir, I think you should have a shower and a shave. By that time lunch will be ready. After that, I think you will be well advised to take three aspirins, and go to bed for an hour or so. I am not yet fully cognisant of the situation, but I am quite sure that unless you get some rest you will not be at your best, and it might be disastrous if you were not competent to cope."

Rollison fingered his grimy stubble.

"Haven't I shaved?"

"Not recently, sir."

Rollison laughed. "I'm much more myself already. All right, I'll do as I'm told. Better hover about while I eat, I can brief you then." He went into the bathroom, caught sight of himself, and whistled. He had a hot shower, followed with a cold one, shaved and got into pyjamas which Jolly had laid out on the bed. He slipped into a dressing-gown of lustrous red silk, and went into the big room, where the dining-table in a small alcove near a window was already laid. There stood a Martini, with the shaker beside it for another if he wanted it. He sipped and smoked.

Jolly came in carrying a tray; and revealed his miracles with lamb chops, sauté potatoes and green peas. Rollison realized that he had not eaten since the previous night, and it was now nearly half-past five.

After the first onslaught, he talked, bringing Jolly up to date with everything. And:

"Then you'd better telephone Miss Gale, and tell her that she won't be hearing from me to-night, after all. Then talk to Grice. I bit his head off and he bit mine, so we're level. He may be co-operative, or he may now put up the shutters. If he's co-operative, I'd like a list of people whom he knows or thinks are on the Doc's payroll. He'll say officially that he hasn't such a list, but reading between the lines I fancy that he's been holding off attacking the small fry, in the hope of catching the Doc. Ask him not to pull anyone in yet if it's possible to avoid it. And if he insists on being difficult," went on Rollison, pulling towards him a bowl of fresh fruit salad and a jug of cream, "reason with him. Use your powers of persuasion. Tell him——"

"I will make the necessary representations to Mr. Grice," said Jolly calmly. "I will tell him that you have a plan."

Rollison chuckled.

"Will you retire now, sir?" asked Jolly.

"Retire?" echoed the Toff. "At my age? Why——"

"I mean, go to bed, sir."

"Certainly not," said Rollison, "I'm going to see Ebbutt and find out what's on in his part of the world."

"You would be much wiser, sir, if——"

"To-night I'm not wise, there's a job to do first," said Rollison. "There's one here, too." He led the way into Jolly's room and unlocked the wardrobe—and there was Galloway, in a kind of stupor.

Rollison spent ten minutes questioning him, without results. Then, his hands and feet still bound, the prisoner was carried into the spare room, and Rollison said to Jolly:

"When you talk to Grice, tell him about Galloway and the egg on top of the wardrobe. Tell him the egg is likely to cause another fire if he isn't very careful, too."

"I will, sir," Jolly said. "But are you sure you should go out again now?"

"Positive," said Rollison. "It's now or never."

He went to the East End, but did not find Ebbutt, who was not at his public house, the Blue Dog, or in the gymnasium behind it—at once his pride and joy. He was said to be out with his wife, but it seemed at least possible that he was avoiding the Toff.

That hurt.

So did the aloofness of Ebbutt's boxing cronies, and others whom Rollison did meet. He sensed that no one really wanted him here, that the Doc had spread his *canard* with telling effect. One thing became apparent; he would have to come back, later in the night, and try again; at least he had learned something of what he was up against.

He drove past Ebbutt's place again on his way home, not knowing that he was within a stone's throw of Dan Rickett.

Rickett was in a small cellar, chained to a wall. He had room to move, and there was a little light, as well as a bundle of straw to sit on. Most of the time he lay flat, staring at the wall, or at his chain; but as Rollison passed, Rickett heard a man approaching.

The door of the cellar opened, and a man whom Rickett had seen several times came in. Rickett did not even glance at him.

"One of these days the Doc will put you where you belong," the new-comer said roughly.

Rickett still ignored him.

"And one of these days your wife will learn about a lot of things she won't like."

Rickett didn't stir.

"Fat lot you think of her," his tormentor sneered, "or you wouldn't let the Doc——"

Rickett turned at last.

"You can't frighten me that way," he said. "If you or the Doc hurt Evie, you wouldn't have a chance in a million of finding out where the stuff is. Remind the Doc about that."

The man swore at him, and then went out.

Rickett gritted his teeth as he stared at his chain. For the moment, it was stalemate, and the Doc wasn't likely to hurt Evie or the baby while he thought he could find those jewels, but sooner or later the stalemate would break.

Rollison was back at Gresham Terrace by eight o'clock. A whisky and soda did little to cheer him up, and Jolly's report depressed him further. Grice had been here, taken Galloway, and gone off in a surly, even hostile mood.

"Well, we'll survive," Rollison said. "What did Miss Gale say?"

"She was out when I called her, sir, and rang through herself a little later, and appeared to be most disappointed that you were out, but I assured her you would get in touch with her at the first opportunity."

"Hmm. That all?"

"Yes, sir."

"All right. I'll have an hour or two's sleep, and then I'm going to see Ebbutt, even if it means dragging him out of bed. I'll do the East End character act, that should fool any friends of the Doc who are interested in our Willum. You get the East End act clothes out—then, unless you're too tired, I've another job for you."

"I slept most of the way on the journey, sir."

"That I don't believe, but I'll let it pass. How many decorated visiting cards have we in stock?"

"A dozen or so, I should think."

"We need more. Embellish a few while I'm lazing in bed, will you?"

"Yes, sir," said Jolly.

Rollison slid down in the bed, and soon relaxed; he had

trained himself to sleep almost at will, and now he was very tired. He had two hours for sleep at the most.

Exactly two hours later, he woke.

His 'East End clothes' were on a chair—a suit old, patched, worn, dirty and dusty. Grease spots decorated the trousers and the lapels. There was a faint but unmistakable odour in it, mingling beer and petrol. Rollison put this on, as if he had never been fastidious, and then put on a pair of old shoes, slightly down at heel, and also patched, and he finished with a muffler which he did up round his neck, choker fashion. He slapped an old cloth cap on the back of his head, studied himself in the mirror, and then pulled it forward.

Satisfied, he took his own automatic, the knife and a small transparent plastic box from the bottom of the wardrobe. This contained little pellets of ammonia gas, fired from a small air pistol. He tucked the pistol away, too, and then went into the study, where Jolly was sitting at the big desk, wielding a pencil almost casually.

Rollison picked up one of the visiting cards that he was 'embellishing'. On one side was the simple legend:

The Hon. Richard Rollison,
22G, Gresham Terrace,
London, W.1.

On the other, in pencil, was a sketch of a faceless man—a top hat, a monocle, a dot for one eye, a cigarette jutting from a holder, and beneath all this a neat bow tie. The drawing was boldly and clearly done.

"I've finished thirty, sir, and there were seven in the drawer," said Jolly.

"I'll take twenty-five, we'll keep the others in reserve," said Rollison. "If I shouldn't come back, let Grice know that I started out to pin Bill Ebbutt down, will you?"

"If you seriously think that there is a risk that you will not return, don't you think——" began Jolly sombrely.

"No, I don't," said Rollison. "I think that I have to handle the Doc as I would anyone else. If I get nervous, he'll find out. If I ask for police protection, he'll hear about it, and my East End stock would be far below zero." He paused, and then went on very softly: "We need to revive our friends' faith, Jolly. We have to be bold and daring, we have——"

"Forgive me, sir," interrupted Jolly, "but you may have overlooked one change in the conditions."

"What change?"

"The passing of years, sir," Jolly murmured.

Rollison's grin broadened, and his eyes kindled.

"Before your very eyes you're seeing the modern Peter Pan," he declared, and rested a hand lightly on Jolly's shoulder. "Of course you're right. So am I. Either I get out of the East End and leave the Doc to the police, or I run true to form. I prefer to run true to form, As I was saying, if I don't come back—or if you haven't heard from me by nine o'clock in the morning, tell Grice."

"*Nine*, sir?" Jolly pleaded silently for eight.

"Eight-thirty," conceded Rollison, and grinned, squeezed Jolly's shoulder, and then turned and left the flat.

14

EBBUTT

THERE were night trains on the underground.

Rollison stepped out of one on the platform of Whitechapel East, and walked towards the stairs and the exit. There were several dozen people on the train, which stopped here for the night. He looked right among them, although as many wore bowlers as wore cloth caps, for there was an increasing white collar job representation among the East End workers. Two couples dawdled, and one of the girls had fair, curly hair, rather like Esmeralda. Rollison wondered what Esmeralda would do next, and whether he was wrong in thinking that she would want to take an active part when she realized that there was trouble.

He couldn't quite make Esmeralda out.

That photograph . . .

The lamps were alight in Whitechapel Road, and one late bus rumbled along the cobbles. The small shops, with the dark, drab windows, were like the shops of a ghost city. Further away, the two and three story houses looked, at this hour of the night, as if they housed the dead. Here and there outside a café or a shop owned by an adventurous individual was a neon sign, but that was almost the only sign of life, apart from the people walking briskly towards their homes. Soon these would go through the little, narrow doorways into tiny, low ceilinged rooms, and the East End would be shut out. They would go to fond wives or to shrews, to mistresses or sluts, to children or to old folk.

None, or very few of them, would think of the Doc—any more than they would think of the Toff or of the police. But it was evident now that the Doc's shadow lay dark upon this land, that the hand of the Doc fell heavily upon the shoulders of many in the East End.

Rollison wished that he knew much more; but he knew one thing beyond all doubt. If he was to throw the Doc back, he must attack now, and in a way which would turn the tide quickly; but before it could be turned, he had to know just how strong it was. There was plenty to disquiet him; and to disquiet many people. The attitude of the police, for one thing, and the fact that Grice—as shrewd an officer as the Yard had—had not realized how bold and ruthless the Doc could be. Grice and the Yard, undoubtedly, had believed that the Doc would start a kind of tribal war in the East End, and that it would end without much help from the police; let a mobster kill a mobster, and pick up the little pieces. It hadn't worked out, and Grice knew, as the Toff knew, that the Doc had a very tight grip indeed.

How tight?

Rollison reached a street which led to the Mile End Road and then, by two short cuts along dark, gloomy, echoing alleys, with cobbles which were snares for the unwary, he went to the Blue Dog, in the Mile End Road, where Bill Ebbutt lived and lorded it; but which he had deserted to-night.

Behind the public house, and taking up much more ground space, was the gymnasium, a large, corrugated iron building where the most likely young boxers of London learned how to take and to give punishment. Ebbutt had a dream: that one day, the heavyweight championship of the world would come to Britain, and he had worked for this dream for over thirty years, getting his nose broken and one magnificent cauliflower ear as a result of it. For twenty years he had trained boxers, and many of the best had started here.

The pub closed, according to the law, at ten-thirty.

The gymnasium, which was also a kind of club, was open until twelve-thirty, and very often Ebbutt and his cronies were there into the small hours, discussing boxing round the world and arguing about the merits of fighters who had passed out of the limelight; or were about to appear in it.

A light was on in the gymnasium now, although it was nearly one o'clock, but there was no noise. Rollison approached it from the mouth of the alley he had come through, and he studied it closely. Was that a man, standing in the shadows outside?

Yes.

It would not have been surprising had two or three men stood there, gossiping; but why should one lurk on his own?

A cigarette glowed, at a level with the face of a normal height man, and showed Rollison that this man was keeping deliberately in the shadows, as if he was watching everyone who went in or out.

Rollison went back to the alley, and the shadows and the safety they offered him.

The light went out in the gymnasium.

There were footsteps, audible right across the street, and made by a heavy man walking on boards which could have been better sprung. Then, in the dim light of the narrow street, the massive figure of Ebbutt appeared, with his huge torso, his double chin, his round, almost bald head; that shone faintly in the light.

Ebbutt turned towards the Blue Dog, which was in darkness except for a lighted window on the first floor. He did not speak to the man in the shadows, but there was little doubt that he knew the man was there. He had only a few yards to walk before he reached the side and private door of the Blue Dog. Rollison heard the key scrape as it went into the lock. The figure in the shadows did not move.

The door closed.

The glow of the cigarette came again, but still the man stood unmoving.

Both doors which led to the Blue Dog were in this street, and could be seen from where the man was standing. So Ebbutt was being watched. Ebbutt was known as a friend of the Toff, was probably known to have been to see him that day.

It would be easy to take the watcher by surprise, and to overpower him; but when he came round he would report in a hurry, and the Doc wouldn't be slow in putting two and two together.

There was another way into the Blue Dog; over the wall which surrounded the gymnasium on the other side, then over another wall into the tiny garden of the pub; then by the garden door, or a window. It would take time and it might make some noise, but it had to be attempted.

Rollison turned back along the alley, went the long way round to approach the gymnasium from the other side, and studied the wall. It was topped with broken glass stuck in cement, but by climbing carefully he got to the top, and jumped. He did the rest by easy stages, until he reached the garden door. A faint smell of beer came from barrels stacked ready for taking away by the brewers dray, and there was a tiny grass patch which Ebbutt's wife tended with almost as much devotion as she attended her Salvation Army meetings at the nearby Citadel.

The light was still on at the back of the pub.

Rollison went to the door, shone a torch on it, and then began to work——

Two minutes later, he was inside the house.

He closed the door without a sound, and then stood by, listening intently, until he was sure that the watching man had heard nothing. Then he shone the torch towards the kitchen door, finding it open. Beyond was a narrow passage, a narrow hall and a staircase. He could see a glow of light upstairs. Now his task was to let Ebbutt know that he was here. He crept up the stairs, and as he reached the top, heard Ebbutt speak in a growling voice.

"Know wot I'm going to do, Liz? And you can ruddy well keep your trap shut; I'm not asking you, I'm *telling* you. I'm going to sell up and buy a country pub. That's me. I'm fed right up wiv London. Why, I'm so fed up wiv London that——"

"Why don't you stop talking such nonsense and go to sleep?" Liz Ebbutt had a tart voice.

"No nonsense abaht it," Ebbutt said aggressively, "that's wot I'm going to do——"

"Anyone would think that there hadn't been a bighead like this Doc before," said his wife sharply. "There've been plenty of them, and look what's happened. They've had their day and then they've got too clever by half, and they're all in prison or else they was hung. Not that I hold with capital punishment; it's a nasty, horrid, barbaric *h*angover, that's what I think of hanging, but you've got to face facts——"

" 'Ere's a fact," Ebbutt said. "I can't step into me own front door wivvout being watched. I can't——"

"Just be patient," Liz said, and there was a gentler note in her voice. "Now listen to me, Bill, you and me's been together for——"

If there was a time for Rollison to reveal his presence, this was it, for what followed might be demonstrative.

And the tone of Liz Ebbutt's voice did not suggest that she was at a screaming pitch of nerves. Rollison went nearer the door, and then said softly but very clearly:

"Much longer than he deserves, Liz."

There was a gasp; a moment of silence; and then a vast creaking of bed springs.

"*What's that?*" gasped Liz.

The springs creaked more until, with a final groaning sound, there was a pause, followed by a thud; Ebbutt was out of bed. Quickly, he rounded the bed and Rollison saw the handle of the door turn and the door open. The light shone out, past the huge ex-boxer, who stood with his hands raised a little in front of him, his mouth open, his eyes rounded with disbelief.

"It *is*," he gasped. "In the flesh, it *is*."

"Why don't you tell me who it is instead——" his wife shrilled.

"It's Mr. Ar," Ebbutt breathed, "it's the old Torf in person. Streuth, Mr. Ar, you dunno 'ow much good this does me. I thought I'd crorsed myself orf the list, I did, strike me pink if I'm not telling the truth. Gorblimey O'Reilly——"

"Hallo, Bill," greeted Rollison mildly.

"Don't you come in here for a minute," called Mrs. Ebbutt hastily.

"All right, Liz," Rollison said, reassuringly. "Bill and I will——"

"And don't you say a *word* until I'm presentable; I want to hear everything," Liz said firmly. There had been a time when she would have refused even to consider talking to him in her bedroom; obviously anxiety had softened her attitude towards him.

Ebbutt was moving forward now. Rollison's hand went out and Ebbutt gripped it tightly enough to hurt; Rollison just grinned. Ebbutt freed him, gulped, ran his hand over his bald head, pulled at his dewlaps, and then gulped again; as full of embarrassment as a child who had been forgiven some major offence.

"There's a cove watching, Mr. Ar, did you——"

"He didn't see me, Bill."

"Then that's okay. Mr. Ar—after I come to see you something—something 'appened. I 'ad to——"

"You can come in," Liz Ebbutt called.

"Mr. Ar," said Ebbutt, in a hoarse whisper, "I 'ope you won't be offended, but the old woman finks as much of you as I do, reelly, so if you wouldn't mind——"

"*And* stop that whispering!"

Ebbutt pushed the door wider open and Rollison went into the bedroom. It was large as rooms went in the East End, and the dark oak furniture was of a quality which showed that the Blue Dog was a paying proposition. The wall-paper and the colour scheme of wine red and pale blue showed that Liz Ebbutt knew exactly what she wanted, and had sound taste. She was sitting up in the middle of a huge bed—its vastness needed for Ebbutt's size—a woman in the late fifties, wearing a pink bed jacket with a fluffy collar of angora wool, a pink night cap adjusted so that only a little of her grey hair showed, and with the wine red eiderdown smoothed out in front of her as if the bed had just been made.

Her dark, beady brown eyes were very bright.

"Glad to see you home again, Mr. Rollison."

"Liz, you get younger every time I go away," said Rollison.

She gave a quick smile. "Well, I don't wonder at it either!"

Rollison chuckled, Ebbutt gasped—and his wife drew back in alarm as Rollison moved swiftly towards her, put his hands on her shoulders, and planted a kiss on either cheek. When he moved away, she had flushed almost as pink as her bed jacket.

"And I've got to say you don't improve any," she declared, "but it's certainly time you got back."

"You mean, it's just what the doctor ordered," murmured Rollison.

She stared, tensely; and then her face puckered into a

grin. Ebbutt gave a snort of sound, and suddenly began to laugh; and his laugh came from deep down. Rollison glanced at the window and saw that it was closed; there was no danger of this uproariousness being heard outside. He waited until the outburst subsided, and it took a long time; when it was over, Ebbutt took a handkerchief from the pocket of his pyjama jacket, and dabbed at his eyes.

"That's the first time I've seen him give a real belly laugh in months," said Mrs. Ebbutt flatly. "You've done him a world o' good already."

"Liz," said Ebbutt, squeakily, "this is one time when I agree wiv you. A proper universe o' good, Mr. Ar, but——" His expression changed, he became grave; and so did his wife. The excitement was over, and cold reason had taken its place, and it wasn't easy to talk about. "Well, I know that's wot you've come to talk abaht, Mr. Ar." He licked his lips, and then said pleadingly: "Caw, couldn't I do wiv a wet!"

"*Beer*," scoffed his wife. "That's all you men ever think of, beer; it's a pity you don't join the Harmy, but I suppose it's too late to be mended now. If you really can't live without it, you'd better go and get yourself a pint. Only one, mind you, I don't mind how much Mr. Rollison has, but only one for you. I," she went on devastatingly, "have got to sleep with you, and I hates beery breath."

"Pint'll do me nicely," said Ebbutt gratefully; "won't be two shakes of a lamb's tail." He hurried out, and moved as quietly as a man could, with a ringcraft which had made him famous in his fighting days.

He made hardly a sound as he went downstairs.

"Mr. Rollison," Liz said quickly and very earnestly, "I got rid of him for a minute because I wanted a word in your ear. Come nearer." She took his hand. "The situation's very bad, believe me, I ain't ever known it worse. I don't know what's come over things, but this Doc, he's a real menace. Got people planted neely ev'rywhere, that's how he works. Cells. Like the Commies. First Bill knew of it, there was a couple of middleweights, seemed good lads to

Bill, but you know what they was doing? Spying on him Then the Doc sent a messenger to Bill, told him he didn't know you any more. Bill sent back a message——"

"Told him to go and fry his flipping face," Ebbutt said, and startled Liz into jumping wildly. Her husband came in carrying a tray with four bottles of beer and two glasses; and a bottle of milk and cup and saucer. Liz faded out of the conversation and Ebbutt took over, while he poured the beer, drank to Rollison's health, and then tipped the milk into a small saucepan and lit the gas at a ring in the fireplace.

"Next day, I was set on. *I* was, Mr. Ar! Caw, they didn't arf smash me up; 'orspitable case I was. The damage was done while I was in the 'orspital, reelly, they got at the boys, scared the lights out of 'em, and scared the lights out of Liz, too. But I wouldn't 'ave given in, Mr. Ar, but for little Lucy—you know, our Maisie's kid. You was at the christening, you remember 'er, she——"

"Three years old with fair curls and a smile like Marilyn Monroe's," Rollison said.

Liz snorted.

"That's her," agreed Ebbutt, and added simply: "She was picked up orf the street this arternoon when I come to see you, Mr. Ar. Neely went mad, Maisie did, and me and Liz—well, what could we do? I 'ad a message that I wasn't to see you no more, or the kid would be a proper mess. I just couldn't take the chance, Mr. Ar, that's the sober truth, I couldn't take it."

"You'd have been wrong to take it," Rollison said quietly.

Ebbutt looked eager.

"You really mean that?"

"Of course I do, Bill. You're to keep out of this—on the surface, anyhow. You don't mind doing a bit of guerrilla work, do you?"

"*Any*fink, Mr. Ar, anyfink at all!"

Ebbutt meant exactly what he said, and his wife supported him; but in fact there was nothing that he must do, after to-night. Rollison was sure of that. If the Doc found out that Ebbutt was helping the Toff, he would act swiftly and viciously, and there would be terrible anguish in this family and greater fear among others. Bill Ebbutt was 'out'. And because of that, Rollison understood more clearly the kind of stranglehold that the Doc had. It was easy to see the pattern; the Doc attacking men who refused, on principle, to go to the police for help, until he had such a hold that they dare not go to the police.

"When did this begin?" Rollison asked.

"Few weeks ago, when the newspapers said you was coming 'ome," Ebbutt told him. "Said you'd leave Noo York in the *Queen 'Liz*, didn't it? Day after, I discovered them two middleweights were the Doc's spies. I put two and two together, Mr. Ar, and guessed the Doc didn't want you to upset 'is arrangements, so to speak. I tried to get in touch with Mr. Jolly, but 'e was out—and after that, when you got back, I just didn't 'ave the 'eart to try to do anyfink."

"You had the good sense not to, Bill. But listen." Rollison drank more beer and leaned back in his chair, while Liz Ebbutt studied him with her beady eyes, and nodded with approval from time to time. "Do you know Dan Rickett?"

Ebbutt was puzzled.

"Well, yus, I know 'im. 'E's not a buddy, but 'e's often come in for a pint."

"Did you know that the Doc snatched his baby?"

Ebbutt didn't speak, but he turned pale. His wife drew in a sharp breath. They hadn't known, but they knew exactly what it meant. Everything they did, almost every word they said, made the ascendancy of the Doc's position more clear.

"Wot 'appened then?" asked Ebbutt, painfully.

"Rickett left the baby at my place," Rollison said. "Then——" it didn't take long to outline the story, and the touching thing was Mrs. Ebbutt's expression when she heard that the child was safe. Rollison stopped talking only long enough to finish his tankard, and to have it refilled, and to light a cigarette. Then he went on: "Any idea why the Doc would try to put pressure on Rickett?"

Ebbutt nodded his great head. "Yus."

"Why?"

"Flyest boy there is in the East End, in the country if it comes to that," said Ebbutt. "He can open anything with a lock, just seems to wave his hands and say *abracadabra*, and the can falls apart. Don't even need a tin-opener! 'Ad a kid brother neely as good, but the kid 'ad trouble with the Doc. He got killed—they *said* it was an accident. All I know is that Rickett said he wouldn't sell to the Doc if he was starving, and he meant it; he hates the Doc. Don't arst me where 'e sold 'is stuff, it wasn't frew any of the reg'lars as far as I know. I got the whisper, you know 'ow it is, everyone talks to everyone dahnstairs over a glass o' beer. There's anuvver whisper, too—did you 'ear abaht the big jewel job in New Bond Street, couple munce ago?"

"No."

"Thief lifted a 'undred thahsand nickers' worth," Ebbutt said flatly. "The Yard didn't 'ave a smell, but I 'eard it was Dan Rickett. Now if the Doc noo it was Rickett and wanted Rickett to sell the stuff to 'im——"

"That's about the size of it," Liz said, quietly, "you don't have to look any further."

Ebbutt said: "What a ruddy swine, I——"

"You may be drinking beer in my bedroom but I'll thank you to mind your language," Liz said tartly.

"Sure, okay, Liz."

"Bill," said Rollison quietly, "I want you to do just one thing. Pass on to me as much gossip about the Doc as you can, and give me a list of all his known contact men. I know there's no direct line to him, but——"

"I can name twenty or more contacts," Ebbutt said.

"Will you make out a list of them? Now?"

"Glad to," said Ebbutt, "won't take two shakes of a lamb's tail, either." He got up from a chair which was much too small for him, and then added almost absently: "You wouldn't like to tell me why you want it, would you?"

"No."

"Quite right, too," said Liz, "the less you know the less you've got to worry about."

"You wouldn't like to tell me something, Bill, would you?" asked Rollison.

"Try me."

Rollison said, very quietly: "I will. Who *is* the Doc, Bill? Do you know?"

There was a long pause, and a quietness in the room, before Ebbutt said very softly:

"No, I don't know 'oo it is, Mr. Ar, but I've got ideas. Lot of uvver people 'ave, too, but you won't get them to talk. Remember, I'm only guessing, but—well, there's a young doctor, come to practise in Mile End a year ago. The Doc wasn't 'eard of until three or four munce after that. It might be just a coincidence, but—well, I'd take a look at Dr. Jonathan Marling, if I was you. Nice chap to look at, but—well, it's a chance, anyway."

"Thanks, Bill," said Rollison. "Now, write that list out for me, will you?"

"Sure," Ebbutt said, "but arf a mo', take a dekko at a picture of Dr. Marling—in the *Gazette* the other night, he was, in the Local Personalities Column. You know."

The *Gazette* was a local newspaper, chatty and discursive and popular. A copy was folded up and tucked in a magazine stand near the bed, and Ebbutt took it out, unfolded it, and pointed to a man's photograph.

"That's 'im," he said. "Looks okay, but 'oo can tell?"

The Toff certainly couldn't tell.

But he felt his heart begin to pound, for this was the man whose photograph had been in poor, dead Maggie's room, and in Esmeralda's handbag.

Soon, he would see Dr. Marling.

15

NIGHT WORK

It was half-past two when Rollison left the Blue Dog, by the same way as he had entered. It was cold, and he shivered in a blustery gust of wind. He went straight to the Mile End Road, and then turned the corner and walked past the gymnasium; he saw the watcher still there, and the light of a street lamp showed him to be in a little porch, where he was sheltered from the wind and where he could sit down. Rollison hunched his shoulders and walked past him.

Half-way along this street was the home of the first man on Ebbutt's list.

Rollison did a simple thing.

He went to the front door, and slipped one of his visiting cards through the letter box, flicking it so that it went a long way into the hall. He let the letter box fall with hardly a sound, and then walked on, whistling under his breath. He went along to the next address, ten minutes' walk away, and as Ebbutt had warned him, found this a builder's home and yard; and in the yard was a bicycle. He borrowed the bicycle, after putting a card into this house, too.

Ebbutt had listed men who lived within a mile or two of the Blue Dog. On a bicycle, Rollison was able to cover them all, and he knew the district as well as he knew the West End of London. He passed one or two night birds, and two policemen, talking at a corner. They didn't ask him what he was doing out so late.

The task took him just over an hour.

The last call was near the Mile End Road, half a mile away from the Blue Dog, and was a hundred yards away from that rarity in the East End, a detached house. This house was on the corner of the main road and a narrower one, and had been built on a spot where four small, terraced houses had been demolished by bombing. In their wisdom the local planning authorities had declared that this was a good position for a doctor to live, and they were truly wise. Rollison knew that an elderly doctor, named Grayson, had lived for years in cramped quarters and with nothing like enough facilities to look after his patients properly. The old doctor's new house had been fully equipped, and two years afterwards, he had taken on a partner—this Dr. Marling.

Dr. Grayson was now dead.

His partner was still there, however, a man of about thirty or thirty-five. Ebbutt had said little but while the list was being prepared Liz Ebbutt had said a lot about Dr. Jonathan Marling. Rollison felt that he almost knew the man, who had certainly known Maggie Jeffson.

Most of what Liz had said was in Dr. Marling's favour.

Rollison pushed open the letter box of the last house on his list, flicked his card in, grinned, stretched himself, and yawned. Then he lifted the bicycle over the wall at the back of the house, and slipped a card between the two halves of the bell. That done, he walked along the Mile End Road.

A red light shone outside the doctor's house.

Rollison reached it.

No lights showed at the windows. A front window was open a few inches at the top, which suggested that Dr. Marling did not fear burglars. There was a low brick wall, a lawn in front and, probably, a vegetable garden at the back of the house.

Rollison vaulted over the wall.

Two cars raced each other along the Mile End Road, going much too fast, headlights swaying up and down. It sounded almost as if it was a police chase. Headlights shone on the house, on the smaller ones nearby, on to the plate glass window of a shop. When the light faded and the engines died away, Rollison was on his own again.

He pulled on some old kid gloves, then examined the

back door, very carefully. It looked simple to open, but that would depend on whether the bolts were shot or not. Rollison couldn't tell without forcing the lock. He turned away and examined the window, using the hooded torch. The stillness of the night lent stealth to his movements. The latch did not seem to be fastened, and he put the blade of his knife beneath the bottom window, and pushed; the window went up far enough for him to get a grip.

The window squeaked as it went up.

Rollison waited, listening, heard nothing, and climbed into the kitchen.

The Ebbutts had told him that a middle-aged man and woman looked after Dr. Marling, who was a bachelor; a bachelor doctor on his own was likely to arouse comment in the East End. Only the three slept in the house, as far as the Ebbutts knew.

Now that Rollison was inside, the risk he took was very much greater. If Marling was an honest man and the rumours against him had no foundation, the fact that the Toff was the Toff, a highly respected citizen, would make little difference in the eyes of the law; unless it made the crime seem worse.

All Grice's influence could do nothing to help him if he were caught.

He went out of the kitchen, walking quietly and slowly. Soon, he had the plan of the ground floor in his mind. The consulting room was at the front on one side, the waiting room across the hall—it was also the dining-room, judging from the furniture. Leading from the consulting room was a little store room and dispensary, where the drugs were kept, some surgical instruments, everything that a doctor and nurse were likely to need.

Beyond this was a small room, which was book-lined from floor to ceiling; a study.

Rollison drew the curtains, after checking that they were not likely to show much light through, closed the door, and then switched on the light of this room. The books seemed to spring at him from the walls. The armchairs were large and comfortable. A bottle of whisky, a siphon and a jar of tobacco were on a small table, next to a copy of the *Times* and one of the popular dailies. Nothing could have seemed more normal.

The books were in great variety. Medical text books filled one wall, classics most of another, translations from the French, German and Italian as well as Spanish, filled two shelves. Marling had a catholic taste in reading. There was a small pedestal desk in one corner, and Rollison sat at this. He hesitated, then stood up and went to the door, listening but hearing no sound.

He put out the light, and opened the door an inch.

No; there was nothing.

He closed the door again, and then went back to the desk. On it was a photograph of a pleasant-faced elderly woman. Marling's mother?

And there was a framed photograph of Esmeralda Gale.

Rollison did not spend much time looking at Esmeralda, but it was difficult to get her out of his mind. There were a lot of questions he wanted to ask Esmeralda——

Later.

The drawer of the desk was locked, but a skeleton key had it open in a few seconds. Rollison opened the other drawers, once this control was free. There was little here. A few letters, some from abroad; pens, pencils, all the oddments a man might have in his desk. There was a folder of bank statements, showing that at the end of June, Marling had had a fairly comfortable bank balance of a little over four hundred pounds. There were some receipts for stock and share certificates, all the investments rather conservative; judging from these, the man was worth about fifteen thousand pounds.

In the bottom drawer were some more photographs; the elderly woman again, this time with an elderly man; two men, youngish and cheerful when the picture was taken; on the back were the words: "George and me, Buxton Conference." There was a family portrait, and several other pictures, mostly of young women—all heads or head and shoulders, all pleasant—all unknown to the Toff.

Except one.

Here was a picture of Margaret Jeffson, otherwise Maggie.

Esmeralda and Maggie, both friends of Marling.

Nothing on the photograph told Rollison why it was here; there was no name, no date, no photographer's stamp. He studied it closely, then looked through and found two others of the same woman. He put one in his pocket, then closed the drawer.

There was nothing else here, no records of names and addresses of the men whom Ebbutt had pinpointed, for instance, nothing to suggest that Marling was leader of the organization which had a stranglehold on part of the East End. There might be something upstairs—or there might be something in the green steel filing cabinet in the office next to the surgery.

Rollison tip-toed to the door again, switched off this light, and opened the door. There was still no sound, and the only light came faintly through a frosted panel of the door; there was a street lamp just outside.

He turned into the office. The window here had a blind, which was down; and he knew that the window faced the garage, so there was less chance of it being noticed. He closed this door, which was facing the foot of the stairs, and opened the cabinet.

The drawer squeaked.

He checked, quickly, and found that the drawer was filled with files dealing with patients; and that it also contained a part of the file of Medical Cards belonging to those patients registered with Dr. Marling under the National Health scheme. The other sections were in the drawer below. Rollison scanned them, picked up the filing system quickly, and then began to check the names on Ebbutt's list. After five minutes, he began to feel a real excitement, for the first seven names of people to whom he had delivered his *billets doux* that night were registered here.

He checked the rest.

His excitement mounted as each one appeared, and by the time he had finished, he found that the twenty-seven people whom Ebbutt knew worked with the Doc were registered with Dr. Marling.

Coincidence?

"Not likely," Rollison murmured, and sat back for a moment, to savour what he had discovered; and to think about it. The one thing he had learned was to take nothing for granted. This might point a finger at Marling, but——

He closed the drawers, one after the other, after making sure that there was nothing else to interest him. He hadn't done too badly, and it might help to find out what kind of reaction there was to the distribution of the cards.

He could come and see Marling to-morrow.

He went cautiously towards the door, listened, heard nothing and opened it. Except for the moment of breaking in, and the visit to Ebbutt, it had been as uneventful a night as he could remember. And welcome. He switched off the light and stepped into the passage. There was just the haze of light against the frosted glass of the door. He might as well go out the front way, it would save climbing a wall at the back, and he would be nearer the main road. He need not walk straight out, but could make sure no police were passing. He had more to worry about from the police now than from anyone else.

He opened the front door a fraction; it wasn't bolted. Most people in Marling's position would have felt safer if the doors were locked and bolted.

He stepped on to the porch, and looked up and down, but saw no sign of the police, no traffic, nothing at all except the shapes of the houses and, a long way down the road, a lighted window and a neon sign. In the distance there was the rumble of heavy traffic, as if several lorries were on the way here. He closed the door with hardly a sound, and stepped out of the porch.

A man, standing close to the wall, struck at him savagely.

Rollison saw the shadowy figure and the upraised arm. He had been so sure that there was nothing to fear that he hadn't a moment's warning. He tried to dodge back, but couldn't. He felt the blow on the side of his head, and it sent him staggering sideways. Before he could recover, the man was on him, smashing blows at his face, his stomach, his chest. And they were powerful, paralysing blows. Vaguely, Rollison realized that he was being attacked by a man who knew where to strike, and how to hurt—a man who seemed intent on hurting more than anything else, because he could have put his victim out in the first few blows.

Why didn't he?

Rollison gasping for breath, covering up as well as he could, felt the blood trickle from a cut in his lips, was vaguely aware of other sounds; and then the rain of blows stopped, and he heard a man's heavy breathing. He himself was crouching against the wall of the house, his hands still covering his face. His right forearm was numb from the blows he had taken on it, his mouth was very sore, and one eye seemed to be swelling.

Then a man said: "Stop that, you ruddy fool! Stop it!"

There was a scuffle, and then the blows stopped and Rollison was aware of two men where there had been one.

"What do you want to do? Kill him?" The newcomer asked roughly.

"He asked for what he got, breaking in here, and——"

"Ever seen him before?"

"Can't say I have, Doc." Rollison's assailant admitted. "If we get him inside we could have a better look at him. Or would you rather call the rozzers?"

The man called 'Doc' had a deep, pleasant voice.

"He's had enough punishment to be getting on with. But I'd like to find out what he was after—my money, or something out of the dispensary. Let's have him in."

"Okay," the other man said.

Rollison knew that if they took him inside and shone a bright light upon him, it would be fatal. This young doctor might be *the* Doc, and if the Doc knew that Rollison was so near, it wouldn't be difficult to get rid of him. He had stopped the other's onslaught, but at a word it could start again, and if a man was killed in a fight when he'd been caught breaking into a house, then——

Marling, who was standing on the porch, was looking at Rollison. Rollison saw a tall, well-built man with dark, curly hair and the face he knew from photographs.

"Come on, get a move on," said the man who had mauled Rollison, "the Doc wants a little talk with you."

"I—I'm coming," Rollison muttered.

"And keep your hands out of your pockets."

"Okay."

The only chance was to fool them; to make them feel that he was finished and there was no fight left in him. He moved away from the door, and then groaned convincingly, and sagged back again, lifting his right leg off the ground. His assailant glanced down.

"Didn't break his leg, did you?" asked Marling abruptly.

"Not me," the boxer said. "Here, stop foxing and take a walk." He pulled at Rollison's right arm.

He was not prepared for any reprisals.

Rollison moved his hand, gripped the other's wrist, and twisted. The man screamed; it was a high-pitched, cut-off sound. Then he crashed against the wall. Half-way down from the porch step, Marling hesitated just long enough to give Rollison a chance to go for him—but Marling was fresh and he'd had warning.

"Don't try to run," he said sharply. "If you do I'll send for——"

Rollison pulled the gas pistol out of his pocket. He was near enough to squirt the gas into Marling's face, to start him coughing and gasping. Marling began to sway as ammonia stung his eyes and nostrils.

The boxer, getting to his feet, unsteadily, gave one long

gasp when Rollison fired another pellet close to his nostrils. Then he began to groan.

Rollison drew back, also gasping.

He saw headlights coming along the road, swaying up and down, the lights of a private car. The beams shone on to the doctor's house and the garden, and would soon shine upon him. He was already clearly visible in the light which came from the hall. He drew back hastily into shadow at the side of the house, but before he reached the corner the car came into sight, and on top of it was the blue and white sign: *Police.*

Police car drivers didn't miss much. They would see the light here, and if they saw either of the staggering men they would come to investigate.

The car slowed down.

Rollison turned the corner of the house, then began to move across the back garden, but his head was throbbing, and he was still out of breath. A whiff or two of the ammonia had blown back at him, his eyes were smarting, and he could feel the gas biting at his nostrils and his mouth; yet he had to keep his mouth open to breathe.

He heard the car engine stop, a door slam, and footsteps. In a few seconds they would see the men on the ground, in a few seconds a police whistle would shrill out.

What chance would he have of getting away?

16

ESMERALDA AGAIN

If he turned and ran, where would he go?

He had no reliable friends nearby; none who would not be too nervous of the police or of the Doc to give him sanctuary. He had the wall to jump, but was in no state to do much running. On this dark night there were police in a hundred places, in doorways, at corners, in cars, waiting and prowling, ready to catch any man who was on the run.

Rollison knew that if he cut and run for it, the odds would be heavily against him.

The two men came running from the police car. He stood close to the corner, peering round, and saw that one was a youthful-looking man, the other a middle-aged Divisional officer whom he knew slightly.

Once that whistle shrilled——

They were only a few feet away from Dr. Marling, who was leaning against the wall, his face buried in his hands, and from the other man on the ground, writhing and pretending to much more pain than he felt.

One of the policemen said sharply:

"That's Dr. Marling."

"Better nip back to the car and——"

They had no time.

Rollison came hurtling from the corner, gun in hand. Each man saw it. For a moment they were petrified with a fear which it was easy to understand, for all they knew this gun was loaded with bullets. One of them flung up his hands, and said harshly:

"Put that gun down!"

Rollison fired a burst at each man's face, then ran on towards the main road and the police car. He could hear them staggering about on the gravel of the path. Once one of them got his breath back he could use his whistle, but that wouldn't be for a few minutes.

Rollison reached the gate.

A big lorry was a few hundred yards down the right road, coming this way.

Rollison said: "Bill Grice, forgive me," and slid into the driving seat. If his luck held, a key was still in the ignition. He felt for it, and found it. His laughter was almost shrill as he eased off the brakes. The engine roared. He drove past a lorry as it came towards him, and watched in his rear mirror once it was past. The driver showed no interest in what was going on outside Dr. Marling's house.

Rollison drove fast, beneath the safety badge of the police sign on the car roof.

A voice came into the car, out of silence.

"Calling Car 39, calling Car 39." There was a pause, and then again: "Calling Car 39, for position and report. Calling Car 39——"

Just visible in the windscreen was the little label, marked 39. The Yard Information Room was calling, and the live radio suggested that the driver had called the Yard, and perhaps reported seeing the scuffle. And there would be several other patrol cars in the vicinity; the quicker he got out of this the better.

"Calling Car 39——"

He knew exactly how the transmission was worked, was almost as familiar with this as with his own Bristol. He flicked the control, and said in a rather hoarse voice:

"This is Car 39, this is Car 39 reporting. Investigating burglary at house of Dr. Marling, Mile End Road, near Rex Cinema. Please send supporting cars. This is Car 39——"

"Calling Car 39," the response came back. "Message received, supporting cars being sent to Dr. Marling's house, Mile End Road. End of message, message ends."

The radio fell silent except for subdued crackling. Rollison drove on, grinning broadly and finding it difficult not to laugh aloud. He was going in one direction, the new cars would be going in the other. Things could only go wrong now if a second car came along this road towards him.

He sobered up.

He saw what he had not noticed before; a faint greyness in the sky. This was the second morning that he had been up to greet the dawn. Buses would soon be running, perhaps they were on the road already. Trains would be running on the tube. He saw three people come out of a street, coats buttoned up against the wind, and turn towards the nearest station—Aldgate East. He turned the car off the main road, and then down a little cul de sac where there were half a dozen small houses. Lights shone from the windows of three of them, but no one was about. He got out, left the car lights on and hurried away from the spot. The footsteps of several people were audible now, and he could hear the whirr of bicycle tyres, as someone came towards him. He had a moment's dread; that this might be a policeman on a bicycle, but he saw that it was someone in a uniformed cap, not a helmet.

He dabbed his cut lip dry, pulled his cap low, and walked off.

He reached Aldgate Station with a little crowd of others. They were shivering in the cold east wind, but he wasn't cold, he was almost too hot. He still wanted to laugh. He could picture Grice's face when Grice learned what had happened; he could imagine Grice jumping quickly to the conclusion that it had been the Toff, but—

Forget it.

He bought a newspaper, glanced at the headlines, and then stopped so abruptly that a man behind cannoned into him. The man grumbled. "Sorry," said Rollison, gruffly, but didn't look up from the *Daily Globe*. There was the whole story of the fire at the hotel and the murder of Maggie Jeffson. The police had kept nothing back; this was one of the few occasions when they had given all known details to the Press, and had obviously asked them to beat the big drum.

The *Globe* had.

So had four other newspapers that Rollison bought, tossing a shilling to the old man at the stall and waiting for his change. A train rumbled nearby, there was a rush from behind him, and he joined in. The train roared into the station and he was half pushed into it. Yet there was plenty of room. He found a corner seat, began to look through the newspapers, and, conscious of the ever-curious eyes of other passengers, he looked at the sporting pages first. He didn't linger on them long.

Four of the front pages starred the Toff, and three carried photographs of him. But the thing which really took him off his balance were the photographs of Esmeralda. She was as photogenic as a Hollywood star, and she smiled up at him with that demure look which somehow wasn't really demure; as if she was intent on making the world think she was.

Rollison put the newspapers down as the train drew into Temple Station. He would get out at Charing Cross, the next stop, and take a taxi. He had not yet fully absorbed the story about the Doc's reign of terror in the East End; and there was the story of the kidnapped baby, of the unnamed thief who had taken it to the Toff for sanctuary. It was all cleverly and smoothly done, and Esmeralda was there because—as she had clearly stated to the newspapers—she had been at Gresham Terrace when the baby had been discovered.

How had the newspapermen got on to her? And what had persuaded her to talk so freely?

"She probably likes seeing her picture in the paper," Rollison said, and made a neighbouring passenger glance at him curiously; the train was now nearly full. Rollison gave a vacant smile, and then glanced at the Stop Press items. Three didn't interest him, but the fourth gave a few more details.

When he reached the street at Charing Cross, and waited for a taxi as a flowing crowd of people went up Villiers Street towards the Strand, he warned himself that the Press would be out in strength at Gresham Terrace. He hoped they wouldn't think of the fire escape.

A taxi driver looked at him suspiciously, but said nothing about his bruised and battered face.

He got out near the approach to the back of Gresham Terrace, and reached the kitchen of the flat at a little after half-past seven. The door was unlocked, which meant that Jolly expected him to come that way. Jolly was moving about further in the flat. There was a smell of freshly ground coffee, rashers of bacon lay in a frying pan, eggs waiting to be cracked, bread waiting to be toasted, a tray laid.

Rollison lit the gas under the coffee percolator, and went into the study.

"And how's the sleepless wonder?" he inquired.

Jolly jumped and half turned.

"I'm sorry, sir, I didn't hear you." His tone suggested that he felt that he had been caught out in a heinous crime but soon he appraised the Toff, and raised one eyebrow when he saw the cut lip and swollen eye. "I hope that cut isn't painful, sir."

"No more than I deserve. Coffee and breakfast first and first-aid afterwards——"

"If you don't mind, sir," said Jolly firmly, "I think that we should bathe that lip at once. We need not put disinfectant on it yet, that would make the coffee unpalatable, but . . ." he dropped into one of his more garrulous moods, which was simply bluff, led Rollison to the bathroom, administered first-aid, and then left Rollison to wash.

When Rollison had finished, breakfast was ready in the window alcove, and coffee was cooling. Rollison took a cup and sipped and looked out of the window, careful to keep to one side so that he could not be seen. There were at least twenty people outside, including several women, and half a dozen of them had cameras.

"How cheap is fame," murmured Rollison, and sat down to his bacon and eggs. "Do you think you annoyed Miss Gale, or is it all my own work?"

"I have to admit, sir, that she did say that she had a very important decision to make, and that she would welcome your advice, and possibly it was a decision about what to say to the newspapers. And we are well aware," went on Jolly in his most pontificial manner, "that newspapermen show a remarkable cunning in eliciting information from people who are not used to their methods."

"Yes. So Esmeralda Gale made a hit with you."

"I am simply looking at both sides of the question, sir."

"Or three sides. Jolly——"

Rollison ate and talked, almost without stopping, and when he had finished there was little that Jolly did not know. The recital served as much to get everything clear in his own mind as it was to keep Jolly informed. When events moved as fast as they had that night, it was easy to get them out of order and out of perspective, and Jolly was adept at getting the right perspective, or at least pointing it out to Rollison.

This time, he said: "I presume you will not use the services that the Ebbutts offered, sir."

"No."

"What was your impression of Dr. Marling?"

"I didn't have time to form one, but I'd like to know why he had a bruiser on the doorstep, as it were." Rollison fingered his lip gently, then got up and looked at himself in a mirror; and to reach the mirror he had to look at the blank wall. He scowled at it. Then he scowled at himself. "In spite of the bruises I'm going to see Marling this morning, then I really will get an impression. And some answers, I hope. I'll see Esmeralda first and Marling soon afterwards."

"I hope you will make that this afternoon, sir," Jolly said. "By that time it might be possible to get some indication of the impact that your cards made on the—ah—Doc's associates. You really cannot manage without sleep, sir. I know," went on Jolly before Rollison could speak, "that you have every desire to be up and about, but I hope you will agree that for the time being it will be better to let things come to the boil—if I may use that simile. You will be much better placed to decide on your next step this afternoon, than you are now."

Rollison looked at him, with his head on one side, and then inquired:

"In what circumstances will you wake me, Jolly?"

"In any justifiable emergency, sir."

"All right," said Rollison, and then yawned, looked out of the window again, and shook his head. "What they will do for sensation. Oh, Jolly."

"Sir?"

"I think I see Ronsey, of the *Globe* down there."

"Do you, sir?"

"Yes. He knows the East End better than most. If you can get at him without letting the other wolves know, ask him if he'll find out if there's been any reaction in the East End—whether he can find out if anything odd happened there last night. Promise him a story later, if he'll dig for us now."

"I'll do that, sir," said Jolly. "I think I am as eager as you to know what happened when your cards were discovered. Good night, sir."

It was then just after nine o'clock.

It was a little after nine o'clock, at a house in Whitechapel, when a tall, lean man with a sneering twist to his lips, got out of bed and scratched his head and then went along the narrow passage to the front door. Newspapers were jutting through the letter box, and there were several letters. Still yawning, he began to pick the letters up, and found that one was just a visiting card. It was dark in the hall, and he couldn't see clearly, but he saw the drawing of the faceless man, and drew in a sharp, hissing breath.

His colour faded.

Half an hour later, he went out, and stepped into the first telephone kiosk. He called a number, and reported; and the man who answered him said:

"That's the *fifteenth*."

"Fif-*teen*?"

"That's what I said."

The man with the sneery twist to his lips said in a flat voice:

"What will *he* say?"

"I don't know how he'll say it, but I know just what he'll say," the other said. "He'll say that we've got to get the so-and-so, to-day. I—hold on a minute, the other phone's ringing, it might be him."

The man waited, in the telephone kiosk, while a few children and several women passed him. It was a quiet, bright morning, with a few fleecy clouds high above the tiny grey houses in the narrow grey streets.

"Vic, you there?"

"Yeh."

"We're to pick up that girl who's spread all over the front pages this morning. See her picture?"

"Yeh," said Vic, "I've seen it. Want me to lay it on?"

"Yes," said the man at the other end of the telephone, "and if I were you I wouldn't lose any time. She's at a flat in Shepherd Market, Number 39. . . ."

The lean-faced man listened, with his right eye screwed up against the smoke from his cigarette.

"Okay," he said at last, "I'll get her."

17

OFFER TO ESMERALDA

THE telephone bell rang in Esmeralda's room.

The flat was a small one in a narrow street which led off Shepherd Market, that tiny village in the heart of Mayfair. She was in the flat alone, for it was after ten o'clock, and the friend who shared this with her left for her office each morning at nine o'clock.

Esmeralda said: "Damn!"

She was sitting cross-legged on a single bed, with the sunlight shining on her from a small window, and it made her hair look lovely and her face quite beautiful. The eagerness in her green-grey eyes gave her a fresh vitality, too, and she kept smiling, a little tautly. In front of her, and all around her, were several newspapers, and she looked from one to another, reading them all. The stop press item fascinated her.

The bell rang again.

She pushed the newspapers aside, and leaned forward to try to reach the telephone without getting up, but it was out of reach. So, she pushed the papers away and slid off the bed. She was wearing a bottle green house jacket, open at the front, and panties and a brassiere, and the little gas fire didn't keep the room warm. She shivered as she picked up the telephone.

"Hallo."

"Is that Miss Esmeralda Gale?"

"Yes." She was almost curt.

"Miss Gale," the caller said, in a rather high-pitched voice, "I'm speaking for the *Weekly Call.* We are very interested in having a story from you——"

"So are several magazines," Esmeralda said, brusquely.

The man chuckled.

"I'm not surprised! But I doubt if you will get any better offer than ours, Miss Gale, we are able to pay extremely well for exclusive stories. We have in mind four or five weekly instalments about this matter between the Toff and the—the Doc—at say two hundred and fifty pounds for each. If that interests you——"

"Well," said Esmeralda, less brusquely, "I can't pretend that it makes me want to ring off. "But——" Her eyes began to shine.

"Knowing how many people will be worrying you," the man said, "we thought it would be wise if we were to come to terms quickly. May I call and see you?"

"When?"

"In a few minutes. I am speaking from a box near your flat. And if it appeals to you, then we can go straight to my office, and make final arrangements."

"Give me ten minutes," said Esmeralda, "and I will certainly talk about it with you. I can't make any promises at this stage, though."

"I quite understand that," said the man with the high-pitched voice. "I'll call on you in ten minutes."

He rang off.

Esmeralda put the receiver down slowly, hesitated, and flung her arms up in the air and gave a little jig.

"I can't help it if Rollison thinks I'm a beast, I knew it would earn a fortune! If he only knew how I *long* to get my hands on some real money. It can't *do* any harm, either."

Then in a flurry of quicksilver movement, she started to dress, putting on a dark red suit. In nine minutes she was ready, and in ten the front door bell rang. The little flat was in a shocking mess, she knew the breakfast things were still on the table in the living-room, and neither bed was made. She put on a black sealskin coat, then a small black hat, picked up her handbag and hurried to the door.

A tall, thin-faced man stood on the step.

"Miss Gale? I'm from the *Call*." He smiled as he spoke, and she didn't particularly like the way his lips curled, but that didn't worry her; she hadn't actually liked any of the men to whom she had talked last evening. "If I may come in——"

"I thought we'd go straight to your office," said Esmeralda, "unless you——"

His smile widened, and he looked pleased.

"Yes, of course, if you're ready to do that. My car's just along the road." It wasn't in the lane, but in the square, a hundred yards away. They walked towards it, passed by some of the villagers, passed a man pushing a fruit barrow and calling his wares.

The car was an Austin Cambridge, with a driver.

Esmeralda got in the back, when the man opened the door. He climbed in after her. She flopped down on the seat, and then eased herself up to straighten her skirt. The man offered cigarettes, and she took one readily, drew in the smoke, and settled down.

"Where is your office?" she asked.

"The main offices are in Fleet Street," the man said,

"but we may have to go to a sub-office afterwards. You're not in any hurry, I hope."

"Oh, no," said Esmeralda helpfully, "I've plenty of time."

It was five minutes afterwards, when they turned into Piccadilly, that she first began to feel tired. She blinked and told herself that she mustn't doze off, she wanted to be at her brightest. But her eyelids seemed to get heavier and heavier, and she started to yawn. It wasn't as if she'd been very late the night before, but the night before that——

Her eyes closed.

Vaguely, she heard the man say: "Okay, Jack, she's off."

Off? What did that mean? She was off? Off where? What was he talking about——

She was off!

He was talking about her, he obviously knew she would soon go to sleep, he had expected it. She was *off*. She forced her eyes open, stared at him, and saw his expression change; he was sneering at her. She tried to get up, but her limbs felt stiff and her body heavy. Her hand touched the handle of the door but slid off it, and the man pulled her back and then held her down on her seat.

Sleep swept over her, killing fear.

Rollison woke.

He could feel pressure at his shoulder, and resented it; he didn't want to wake. But the pressure was insistent, and he was being shaken firmly. This would be Jolly. He was snug and warm and his eyes were so tightly closed that he knew he hadn't had anything like enough sleep; he must get rid of Jolly. It was no use him walking about like a sleep-walker.

". . . is waiting, sir," Jolly said, as if from a long way off.

". . . really important, sir."

There was a moment's pause, as Rollison tried to open his eyes, and then Jolly stopped shaking him, and there was a different sound, at the door; a different voice, too.

"All right, Jolly, I'll wake him."

That was Grice.

Rollison worked his arms out of the bedclothes, and slowly held them up, as in a token of surrender. Then he began to hitch himself up; yawning. There was a clink of cups. He blinked at Grice, who stood at the foot of the bed, tall and good-looking in his sallow, tight-skinned way, his expression quite neutral. Jolly was pouring out tea. Bless Jolly.

"Thanks," said Rollison, and took a cup. He sipped, then squinted up. "Morning, Bill."

"It's half-past two."

"Afternoon, Bill."

"Where were you last night?"

"Out."

"Whereabouts?"

"Just out."

"Exactly what were you doing?"

Rollison sipped again, put the cup and saucer on a bed-side table, and waved his hands and smiled amiably. Then he wished he hadn't, for his split lip stung, and he winced. But he still waved his arms, and said:

"Burgling houses and things."

"For once I believe you. What made you break into Dr. Marling's home?"

Rollison stared. "Whose?"

"You heard me."

"The trouble is that I haven't heard of the doctor you spoke of, as far as I recall. Marling, did you say?"

He picked up his cup again, and retained a bland expression, but he was by no means sure that he could get away with this. Grice had jumped to the right conclusion, and if Grice thought that it would help, he would drive his accusation home; provided he had any evidence. Had he? It was conceivable but unlikely that the Toff had been recognized, but——

Forget it.

Grice was alone, which meant that he didn't want any official notice taken of what he was saying. So this visit was not really ominous.

"Yes," Grice said, "I meant Dr. Marling. He is feeling pretty mad about a man who broke into his house, and afterwards attacked him with ammonia gas. So are two of my men, who had the same treatment and whose car was stolen——"

"*Police* car stolen?" Rollison gaped. "Surely——"

"All right," said Grice, "I doubt if I could prove it, even if I tried. Stop fooling, and listen. How well do you know Esmeralda Gale?"

"Hardly at all."

"Is that true?"

"Absolutely true. I met her at a cocktail party—but I've told you all about this," protested Rollison.

"I know," said Grice, "and now I think I believe you, so it shouldn't make a lot of difference to you. She's missing."

"*What?*"

"She left her flat this morning with a strange man, was driven off in a dark blue Austin Cambridge, and hasn't been seen since. She was to have lunched with her aunt, Mrs. Wylie, but didn't turn up. Where is she?"

Rollison didn't speak.

"I know that she put a spanner into your works when she talked so much to the Press," Grice said, "but that doesn't mean that you can hide her away and——"

"Wrong," said Rollison, and he knew that Grice would need no more telling that this was the truth. "I don't know where she is. I haven't seen her since she was here, and—are you sure about this?"

"Positive."

"But she can't have been gone long——"

"That isn't the point. She was to have seen her aunt, and it was an important matter. Do you know much about Miss Gale?"

"Hardly a thing, except that she wouldn't exactly frighten me on a dark night."

"She is the daughter of a wealthy man who died heavily in debt," said Grice, "and she was left without training for any job, without any way of earning the kind of living she was used to. You probably know that. She's an independent type, and wouldn't take too much charity from her aunt and uncle, so got along on her own. Wylie thinks she told the press about this for what they'd pay her. He's pretty mad about the way she talked, you can imagine that he doesn't relish the newspapers this morning. He hasn't approved of a lot of the things she's done. The luncheon with her aunt was to talk about that, and she wouldn't be likely to cut it deliberately."

Rollison finished his tea and said: "Probably not." He pushed back the bedclothes, and got out of bed. "Ugly. Any ideas, Bill?"

"Not about Miss Gale." Grice hesitated, as Rollison began to dress, with Jolly handing him his clothes. "I can only say that if she is in the hands of the Doc, I wouldn't like to say what will happen to her." Grice didn't raise his voice, and that made his words sound even more ominous. "You know the kind of thing the Doc's been doing, now, and I've a clearer picture. I picked up several of the boys last night, and they told me more about the Doc than I wanted to hear."

"Get anything out of Galloway, the man who was here?"

"No more than you did," Grice said.

"What about Penn—the chap your fellows held in Throgmorton Square when the Rickett baby was kidnapped?"

"He won't talk at all," said Grice. "The general picture is identical, though. They contact the Doc at telephone numbers which are changed frequently, or they meet other men by appointment—as Galloway met the man who was with him at your flat—each having the same instructions. The Doc doesn't exactly trust his followers."

"Wisdom in villainy," Rollison said. "What about that egg?"

"It's still being studied at an Army Research station," Grice said. "All I know is that it's made up partly of flame thrower oil, with a detonator to set it off on the concussion principle. A kind of hand-grenade."

"One word," Rollison said. "Alarming."

"That's it. And that's why I'm talking to you, and that's why I'm asking you if you've any reason to believe that Dr. Jonathan Marling is associated with the Doc. Never mind whether you were there last night, or what reason you have for suspicion—just tell me whether you suspect him? If you do——"

There was a sharp ring at the front door of the flat, repeated almost before the echo had died. Jolly, hovering in the doorway, moved round; Grice, the thread of what he was saying broken, glanced at the door with annoyance, Rollison was now dressed except for collar, tie and coat.

The sound of Jolly's footsteps across the flat faded; the door was opened.

Then: "*Oh!*" exclaimed Jolly, in a voice which seemed loaded with alarm.

Rollison was as near the door as Grice, and reached it a foot in front of him, brushing against him as he went out. He heard another man—realized that there were several people coming into the flat. He was prepared for anything; for the frontal attack which could quite easily come from the Doc—but there was Jolly, and if Jolly was in acute danger——

"Careful with her," a man said gruffly.

Rollison reached the door through which he could see what was happening; and he froze to a standstill. Jolly was backing away from the open door. Several men, two of them carrying cameras, were outside, two were coming in —and between them they carried a woman.

Rollison didn't recognize her.

She was half-conscious. Her face was bruised and battered. Some of her hair had been pulled out. Her clothes were torn. The two men who made a chair for her carried her gently across to a big couch, and laid her on it. As they did so, Rollison saw the cards which were pinned to her clothes.

They were his cards; the cards he had delivered the night before.

18

THREAT

As the men put the woman down, she groaned. Rollison was already moving to the bureau where Dan Rickett had left his note and so begun all this. He lifted the telephone and dialled a number. Men streamed into the flat, and cameras were raised, flashlights made the room bright. There was a hum of talk, outside and inside the flat, but Rollison was oblivious of most of this. He studied the injured woman and the cards, and listened to the dialling sound.

He was answered. "This is Dr. Harrison's residence."

"Is Dr. Harrison in?" Rollison asked. "It's Richard Rollison here."

"Yes, sir, I'll put you through."

"Ask him to come across to my flat at once, will you?" asked Rollison. "An accident case." He put down the receiver, and went quickly across to the woman. She had stopped moaning, and was looking about her. Jolly was coming from the bathroom, carrying a bowl of water and a sponge. Grice was standing over the couch, as if forbidding anyone to come nearer, but no one tried. More cameras clicked and flashed as Rollison drew near.

The woman was staring up at him.

"You—you—you're Mr. Rollison," she said, in a husky voice, as if it hurt her to speak. "You—you're the Toff."

In spite of the bruises, in spite of the bleeding, he recognized her. He had seen her photograph at Rose Cottage, where her mother and her father had been murdered. This was Evie Rickett, mother of the baby whom the police were looking after. She began to shiver, and someone said: "Bring a blanket," but Rollison only heard that as if it had been uttered a long way off.

"Yes, I'm Richard Rollison," he said, and went down on one knee beside the woman, and smiled. "I've some good news for you."

She stared at him, her face puckering.

"*Good* news?"

"Very good," he assured her, "your baby is quite safe and quite well. He's in a nursing home, with a strong police guard. You will be with him soon, too."

She tried to sit up, although obviously movement hurt her. She gripped his hands tightly, and seemed as if she meant to pull him towards her. Her eyes blazed with an indescribable radiance.

"Is that true, is—is Baby——"

"Quite safe. Quite well."

"Oh, thank God," she said, "thank God."

Then, she began to cry, sinking back on to the cushions and putting her hands to her face; and it seemed as if she would never stop crying. Jolly came back with the blanket, and one of the women newspaper reporters came forward and picked up the sponge and wrung it out. Rollison hadn't noticed their going, but several of the others had gone, now, in a rush to their newspapers or telephones. Two policemen had arrived, and were at the open door.

Grice touched Rollison's shoulder.

"Yes, Bill?"

"You'd better handle her," Grice said. "I shouldn't think she's dangerously hurt, and if we can get a statement before she's taken to a nursing-home——"

"No nursing-home, unless it's essential—she stays here," said Rollison gruffly. "I think the injuries are superficial, too. Just to impress us. How the devil she got here——"

"I've just been told," Grice said, "she was thrown out of a car at the end of the street. A reporter chased the car, we haven't heard whether it has been traced yet. She kept saying the same thing over and over again, she had to see you, it was a matter of life and death, and the newspapermen decided they'd better bring her up."

"Good thing she wasn't worse than she is," Rollison said. He spoke almost absently, while taking out cigarettes. "Here's Harrison, we'll soon know the score." He went to the doorway to greet a middle-aged, bullet-headed man dressed in dark grey, and who carried a large black box-like case. He had florid cheeks and bright blue eyes, and seemed to regard everything that he saw here with complete equanimity.

"Thanks, Charles," Rollison said. "Here she is. I'd like her to stay here, if a nurse is all she needs for a bit, and we'd like her to talk."

"Really matter?"

"Yes."

"All right," said Harrison, and went across to Evie Rickett, who was still crying.

Twenty minutes later, she looked better. Her face had been bathed and the bruises and the cuts treated. She was a mass of sticking plaster, but no stitches had been necessary. Her hair was drawn back from her forehead, throwing her pleasant features into sharper relief. Jolly had taken the cards from her dress, one by one and with great care, and they were on the bureau. Two C.I.D. men had arrived, and Grice was giving them instructions—to look for the reporter who had followed the car, and to have the cards tested for fingerprints.

Harrison said: "No reason to move her, get her into that spare room of yours, that's all. I'll arrange for a nurse——"

"We'll do that," Grice said, quickly.

"Please yourself," said Harrison, "all that matters is that she feels secure. In spite of Rolly here, I'd have guards back and front, and a couple on the roof if I were you."

"Thanks," said Grice, dryly. "I will."

Rollison said: "Thanks, Charles, you're always on the spot." Then he forgot Harrison, and turned back to the couch. Evie Rickett's swollen eyes and puffy lips would have told their tale without the cuts and bruises; but she was much calmer, and didn't hesitate to speak.

"You won't let anything happen to Baby, will you? You won't let him be—be taken again."

"You haven't a thing to worry about with him," Rollison said, "he's as safe as the Crown Jewels."

He won a smile.

"I'd like to know what happened to you after you left here," he said gently. "Will you try to tell us?"

She hesitated. Tears were very close to her eyes, and Rollison wondered whether she would be able to bring herself to talk; but gradually she began, and the story unfolded graphically and in a way which made all the people present feel a deep and bitter hatred towards the man who had caused this suffering.

She did not say that she knew her husband was a crack burglar, or that he had the proceeds of a big robbery hidden away. She just said that the Doc wanted something from him, and he would not give it up. The Doc had threatened the baby, and:

"We just had to get him away," Evie said, "we knew the Doc's men were after us, and we couldn't get far. Dan said you'd see that Baby was all right, he said he'd back you against the Doc any day, so we brought him to you, and——"

She broke off, choking.

No one spoke, before she went on:

"Then we had to get down to my Ma and Pa, at Guildford, we was flat broke, and we knew they'd lend us a bit of ready. Dan was all for getting out of the country, but——"

She nearly broke down again.

Gradually, the whole story came out. The old couple getting the money from a hiding-place, while Dan Rickett was working on the motor-cycle, which had been missing badly. Desperately anxious to make sure that her child was all right, Evie had called Rollison.

"And then Dan started blowing his horn, so I knew

something was up. A car came up, nearly crashed into Dan it did, and men jumped out and come at me. My mum tried to stop him——"

The men had killed both the old folk, and carried her and Dan away, with the motor-cycle fastened inside the boot of the big car. She hadn't seen Dan since they'd been taken out of the car an hour or so later, blindfolded so that they could not see where they were.

Now the story was told, Evie looked so white that she might faint at any moment.

"Evie, just tell us this," Rollison said. "Where have they kept you?"

"I don't know," Evie said wearily, "it's been in a big cellar, that's all I know, I think it was beneath a pub." She paused again, and pressed the heels of her hands into her eyes. "There was a smell of beer and spirits, you can't mistake it, I—but what does it matter? They kept threatening Baby, they said if they couldn't make Dan do what they wanted, they'd kill Baby."

"What do they want so badly?" asked Rollison.

Evie's reddened, roughened hands clenched, and her shoulder squared. She looked at him levelly, and it was obvious that she had no thought for herself, only for her husband. She looked at Grice and at the two policemen, swift, fleeting glances, and then she said with great deliberation:

"It's no use asking me, I don't know."

She knew.

She would probably deny it even under threat of death, but she knew that her Dan was a thief, she knew that he had made a big haul which the Doc wanted from him; but she would not betray her man.

"All right," said Rollison, and smiled as if he believed her. "What else can you tell us, Evie? Have you seen any of the men at this place that smells like a pub?"

"No, they—they put some drops in my eyes, I couldn't

see, it wasn't until this morning that I could see," she said, "and then they put a bandage round my eyes. Someone took it off after I was thrown out, and——"

"That's right, sir, according to a statement I was given," a policeman said to Grice.

Grice nodded.

"What's the point in me lying?" asked Evie Rickett, and she looked almost scornfully at the speaker. "I just haven't seen anyone, Mr. Rollison. It's no use asking me. If—if I could do anything to help you catch the swine, do you think I wouldn't?"

"You'd help," Rollison said, and hesitated before he asked her: "Did you have to bring any message for me?"

"Yes," she said, huskily.

"What was it?"

She drew a deep breath.

"I was to tell you that if you didn't throw your hand in, Esmeralda Gale would get a lot worse than I got. That's the message, that's all I can tell you." Evie drew back, now, and closed her eyes and her voice dropped to a whisper. "I can't talk any more, I just can't talk, but—I want to see my baby. Please can I see my baby?"

19

ALLEGATIONS

THE flat was quiet, as Grice and Rollison eyed each other, across the big desk.

Evie Rickett was asleep in the spare room, with a police nurse waiting by her side, ready to take down anything else she said, and to give her any help she needed. Outside the house, both back and front, there were C.I.D. men. All the newspapermen and women had gone, and their legacy would be in the early papers. Grice had spent some time on the telephone to the Yard, and Rollison knew that much of the time he had been talking to the Assistant Commissioner.

The *Globe* man had telephoned to tell Rollison that the East End was agog with the news that the Toff was fighting back, and the story of the visiting cards was the best joke for years.

There was laughter, now, against the Doc.

He wouldn't like it. He would sense the danger behind it. He had pinned those cards on to poor Evie Rickett and sent her to Rollison, hoping to make Rollison hold his hand, fearing harm to others.

The Doc was on the defensive at last.

And he'd kept Evie in the cellar of a pub.

"Well, what's on your mind, Bill?" Rollison asked. "Am I ordered to keep my hands off the job?" There was a glint in his eyes. "Because nothing you could say would stop me, and little you could do."

"I'm not sure that I want you off the job," Grice said. "The Doc wants that, so why should I?"

"Nice logic."

"Rolly," said Grice, "there are one or two things that you probably don't know, and at least one you won't agree with me about."

"We might compromise," murmured Rollison.

"Not on this. First—I don't believe that any man would do what the Doc is doing, unless he intended to finish it quickly. He would know that he can't stage what amounts to a reign of terror and get away with it for long. A few days grace is the most he can hope for. He's got this collection of contact men who do exactly what he tells them, and he covers his traces with most of them, but someone must know who he is. The woman Jeffson must have been killed because she knew him, or else could give us an idea where to find him. He's been working quietly and thoroughly, and he's got a stranglehold on many people, but this open clash with us is something different. Either a crisis had been forced upon him, or one has developed beyond his control. I think he will probably stop this killing once the crisis is over. Agree?" Grice flashed.

"Up to a point," Rollison said. "I think he might be staging this simply as a demonstration. If he can challenge the police openly and get away with it once, his influence will grow much stronger. And it's already strong enough."

"Could be," agreed Grice. "Now, look at our point of view. We daren't let him get away with it. We must catch him, and we're going to. I think we can do it quicker with your help."

"Thanks," Rollison said. "How?"

"You haven't told us why you suspect Marling."

"He was named last night as a possible Doc."

"Who named him?"

"An old friend of mine."

"I thought so," Grice said, and he smoothed his chin, while his look gave Rollison the impression that he didn't relish what he was going to say next. "Was it Ebbutt, of the Blue Dog?"

"Yes."

"How did he come to suspect Marling?"

"It's on the local grapevine."

"Listen, Rolly," Grice said very tensely, "your mind is usually as sharp as they come, what's blunting it now? You know that the Doc is unknown to everyone. Very few of his own contacts have any idea who he is. How do you think Ebbutt or anyone else can get hold of a rumour like that?"

"Ebbutt keeps his ear to the ground," Rollison said.

"Yes," snapped Grice, "and he may keep a lot more underground. I know that he's a friend of yours, but I also know that he isn't a friend of ours. He's run that boxing business of his for over twenty-five years. He's had thousands of people through the gymnasium, and half of them have been men just out of jail, or men who ought to be in jail. We've suspected for a long time that it's been a clearing house of crime—whether Ebbutt was aware of it or not."

Rollison was sitting very still.

"Go on, Bill."

"I'm going on. We've been investigating the affairs of that gymnasium and that pub very closely. Ebbutt's got a remarkable lot of money. He will often give young boxers well-paid jobs at the gymnasium, just to train them. He has a kind of pension list for old boxers and that must cost him a fortune. As nearly as we can estimate, Bill Ebbutt has a payroll of over two hundred pounds a month. Think the profits at the Blue Dog cover that?"

"No," said Rollison, softly.

"I'm glad I don't have to open your eyes all the way. Now take another look at Ebbutt. He's been carving a niche for himself for a long time. He's the big shot around there, because of the boxing and the gymnasium. He commands a great deal of loyalty. He may have started off with the idea of running a good show for boxers, but the power he got through it may have gone to his head. Once a man's had a taste of power, especially a strong-willed man like Ebbutt, you can't be sure how far it will go. Ebbutt's persuaded you that he's being victimised by the Doc, but —is he? Supposing he *is* the Doc?"

Rollison's lean hands were on the desk, and they were very still. His eyes were narrowed, and his face set. He didn't speak, and he didn't move.

"If he is, he'd want to put you on the wrong track, wouldn't he? He would want to make it look as if he was being victimised. And he would want to keep friendly with you. Remember you, as the Toff, have given Ebbutt a lot of protection for years. You've always trusted him. Whenever you've wanted an under-cover job done, a job that the police wouldn't do, whenever you've wanted strong arm help, you've called on Ebbutt. He's given it to you, and he's established himself as a buddy of the Toff, and therefore he must be trustworthy. Supposing he *isn't*, Rolly. Supposing the gymnasium and the Blue Dog together make up the clearing house for the Doc's messages. How would that fit in with the general scheme of things—including the fact that Mrs. Rickett says she was being held at a pub, or where there was a smell of beer?"

Rollison stirred. "It would fit in," he conceded.

"Some other things would, too," went on Grice. "We've been watching for a long time, you know that. We thought that we could catch the Doc before he did any real harm—that he was doing more good than harm by setting the crooks and the fences against one another, but that doesn't mean that we haven't kept our eyes open. And most leads we've got have taken us to the Blue Dog and Ebbutt, *not* to Marling."

Rollison put his hand to his pocket, took out his cigarettes, and proffered the case to Grice. Grice seldom smoked, but he seemed glad of a cigarette now. Rollison flicked his lighter, and they lit up; everything was done with great deliberation.

"What is your brief for Marling?" Rollison asked, at last.

"I've no brief for him, but surely you can see——"

"The obvious," Rollison interrupted, and he smiled but could not command the wanted lightness of tone or of expression. "That it would pay the Doc to allow false rumours to spread. As you've said. That it is much more likely that a man of Ebbutt's dominating personality and his intricate knowledge of the East End would lead this business, than would a youngish doctor who's only recently gone to live in the place. Yes, I can see all that. I can't see Ebbutt as a king pin in this, though. I can only see Ebbutt as an honest man."

"Paying out two hundred pounds a month in wages which you might almost call pensions."

"Yes," said Rollison, "I know."

"Where do you think he gets his money from?"

"I think Ebbutt's been a careful business man all his life, and that he's comfortably off," Rollison said. "And if he pays these wages, he doesn't pay tax on the money.

But all right, Bill. Ebbutt is your Suspect Number 1. I haven't one yet—Marling is only an outsider."

He didn't think that this was the moment to tell Grice that Marling's photograph had been in Maggie's apartment, or that Esmeralda Gale was also involved with Marling. Grice would not have taken this anti-Ebbutt line unless he felt that it was essential, and it had to be probed, deeply.

"What are you going to do?" Grice asked.

"I'm going to see Marling first, and then I'm going to look for Esmeralda," Rollison said, "but I'm not going to find her—not yet. The Doc will tell me where to find her, soon enough."

Grice said: "I don't follow." The look of strain had gone, obviously he was relieved that Rollison accepted even the possibility that Ebbutt was the Doc. "Why should the Doc tell you——"

"He'll get word to me that Esmeralda is in a certain place," said Rollison, "and he'll say that if I go there he might make terms. He'll take a chance on my known reputation for preferring to work with Ebbutt and his cronies than the police. He'll bait his trap with Esmeralda, and I——"

Grice said sharply: "What will you do?"

"Walk into it."

"Don't be a fool! If ever there was a case for working along with us, this is it. We'll give you all the protection you need, and you——"

"You've plenty of people to look after," Rollison said mildly. "I'll look after myself."

Grice drew in a deep breath, but didn't attempt to persuade him.

Grice had gone.

Jolly came in from the kitchen, where he had undoubtedly been waiting and listening, with the door ajar. He looked as sedate as ever, and gave no inkling of his thoughts until Rollison said:

"How far do you go along with Grice, Jolly?"

"If Ebbutt is the—ah—person known as the Doc," said Jolly, very softly, "it will be the great surprise of my life, and I would immediately advise you to withdraw from all contact with the East End of London and with all investigation of crime. If you—if *we* could be so wrong——"

"We shall retire together," declared Rollison, "and take a pub in the country." He paused. "Jolly, I visited Ebbutt last night. I interrupted a conversation between him and Liz. I heard him as dispirited as a man could be. He talked of selling up and going to live in the country. At the time, I thought he was down in the dumps, because obviously he'd been under pressure, but could he have known that I was in the pub? Could he have heard me getting in, guessed who it was, and timed his little chat with his wife?"

Jolly eased his position.

"I suppose it is conceivable, sir," he said, "and if there is any justification at all for Mr. Grice's allegations, then there is at least one supporting factor which I'm sure you have already seen."

"Tell me about it."

"I was very puzzled indeed when Ebbutt said that he would not come to your assistance the other night," elaborated Jolly, "and in the light of what we have now been given to understand, it is at least possible that he was pretending to be frightened, but that in fact——"

"If a man's wife and grandchild are threatened with injury and perhaps torture, I think most men can be frightened."

"No doubt, sir," conceded Jolly, "but Ebbutt is a very strong character indeed. He has always been strong-willed, obstinate, and aggressive, and—but I think it would be better to try to judge by results, sir, don't you?"

"I do," agreed Rollison, "and now I'm really going to see Marling."

"May I ask which suit you require, sir?" asked Jolly.

Before he left, Rollison looked in to see Evie Rickett.

She was in a drugged sleep; and all the injuries showed up on her tired face.

Rollison seemed to see another face; Esmeralda Gale's.

There was no sign of the struggle outside the doctor's house in the Mile End Road, when Rollison arrived there. He had parked a hired car, a cream-coloured Jaguar, right opposite the front door, in full view of everyone passing. Traffic was thick and fast, but the wide road allowed plenty of room for parking. The red lamp was not alight. The grass looked very green and beautifully trimmed. The house itself was no thing of beauty, being of yellow brick which had not lost its harsh newness, but it had a spaciousness and a solidity which most of the buildings in the vicinity lacked.

A middle-aged woman with dark hair and the colouring of a Southern European, opened the door.

"Is Dr. Marling in, please?" Rollison said, as she smiled a welcome.

"Please, who wishes him?"

"Will you take in this card?"

"Immediately, sir." Her accent was attractive. She moved to one side of the hall and tapped at a door and went straight in; it was the door of the surgery.

She came out almost at once.

"Please, wiz me," she said. She did not lead the way to the surgery, but to the room where Rollison had found the picture of Maggie Jeffson. She closed the door on him, and the carpet which covered rooms and passages from wall to wall muffled all her footsteps. Rollison waited until she had had time to go, and then opened the door a crack, and listened; Marling might be on the telephone, might be sending for—whom?

There was no sound of a voice, and in a moment the surgery door opened. Rollison backed away, without closing his door. Marling's footsteps grew firmer and heavier; he was approaching, and could hardly have had time to telephone or to speak to anyone else.

He pushed the door wide open and came in.

Rollison's impression of the night before was strengthened. Here was a tall, good-looking man, with a strong face, an easy, self-confident smile, black, curly hair. He wore a beautifully cut suit of navy blue, and looked immaculate; the East End practice didn't pull him down at all. He had lithe, easy movements, too. Rollison noticed all these things, and yet the thing that impressed him most was the look in Marling's eyes; a smile that couldn't be mistaken.

"Mr. Rollison?"

"Yes."

Marling held out his hand; the grip was firm and the hand cool.

"I nearly called you the Toff," he confided. "I don't know of a man I've heard more about—mostly to your credit!" He motioned to a chair and took out cigarettes. "I don't think we'd met until last night, had we?" he added, and the smile was gay in his eyes and the lighter steady in his hand.

Rollison said mildly: "I don't even remember meeting last night." He gave Marling a chance to come back at that, but the doctor let it pass. They sat down. "Dr. Marling, I know you're a busy man and I won't waste your time. Will you answer a few questions?"

"If I can, and if they don't incriminate me!"

Rollison studied, liked and even admired him; and that was a great deal to have decided in a few minutes. It wasn't just because of the man's appearance or his smile, it was his poise and self-confidence too.

"I don't think I want you to incriminate yourself," said Rollison, "all I want is to find out if you have any idea who the Doc is. *The* Doc," he repeated, "and I'm not thinking medically, it's just a nickname."

"I know which Doc you mean," said Marling, without a moment's hesitation. "Whether I suspect who he is——" he shrugged. "I don't like guessing, especially on such a subject, and in any case so much of what I hear comes by way of professional confidence that it isn't easy to answer everything I'm asked. But you know that."

Rollison said mildly: "Yes, I know. Have you read the newspapers this morning?"

"Several of them."

"Did any of them have a photograph of Miss Jeffson, who was shot and murdered yesterday?"

"No." Marling looked puzzled but not uneasy.

"I didn't see her picture in the newspapers either," said Rollison, "but I came across one, and you might be interested in it." He took out the photograph he had taken last night.

Marling took one look, and his whole manner seemed to change. The smile faded from his eyes, and shocked horror replaced it. His lithe body lost its suppleness, and he seemed to be rigid, as if there had been some physical transformation.

He stared down at the picture, his jaws working.

Then, he looked up.

20

WHISPERS

ROLLISON thought that the other man would strike him. What relationship had there been to cause such an effect as this—relationship with a woman whose name he did not know.

Name, or *alias*?

The glitter in Marling's eyes held a kind of menace, and his hands clenched by his sides. Something stopped him from speaking; perhaps it was the shock, coming right out of the blue.

Then, he said harshly: "You sure?"

"I was with her when she died," Rollison said.

"Why?"

"I'd discovered that she worked for the Doc."

"Meg did *that*," said Marling, and closed his eyes. After a moment he turned round abruptly and pressed a button in one of the bookcases; a small cupboard swung open, and inside there were glasses, whisky, brandy, gin, soda, vermouth. Marling poured himself a brandy, and drank it too fast. Then he waved towards the drinks.

"You?"

"Not now, thanks. Who was she?"

"Meg," said Marling, and gave a laugh that was almost a cry. "My sister. My twin sister. Oh, my God! You—listen to me, Rollison. You must be mistaken. I just don't believe it!"

"Her face isn't badly scarred, and they will let you see her," Rollison said gently. "She was taken to the morgue at Cannon Row, close to the Yard. But don't deceive yourself, Marling. She worked for the Doc, and he killed her." He paused, but Marling didn't speak, seemed to be fighting to regain his self-control, so he went on: "I'll tell you some other things. I've been trying to find out who the Doc is. I've heard whispers, and they're all the same. That you're the Doc. *The* Doc."

Marling growled: "That's why you came here last night."

"Never mind last night."

"Whoever says it is lying and I'll ram the words down his throat."

"Let's go on from there. You keep talking about last night. I know what happened then, and I know you had another man here, a man useful with his fists. Who is he?"

"Luke Dalton? He's odd job man here, I've just taken him on. Chauffeur, mechanic, general worker. In fact he's a damned good middleweight boxer." Marling looked pointedly at Rollison's chin. "He's training now, and spends part time with me. He heard you about last night, and decided to teach you a lesson."

Marling seemed to believe that.

"Who is he training with?" Rollison asked.

"Your friend Ebbutt. Your friend *Ebbutt*," Marling repeated. He snatched a glance at the photograph of Meg, his sister, then went on savagely: "You talk about whispers, naming me. Why don't you keep your ear to the ground? Why don't you hear what they're saying about Ebbutt?"

Rollison thought, coldly, miserably: 'The only whispers I pick up about the East End come from Ebbutt.' But he didn't say that. "Well, let's have it," he said.

"They're saying that Ebbutt has fooled you for years," Marling told him, and there was bitterness but no malice in his voice. "Let me be perfectly frank, Rollison. I'm prejudiced in your favour. I've read and heard about you for years—I've a young brother who hero-worships you. I've followed your career very closely, partly because the East End of London had always fascinated me. I like the Cockneys, I think they're the salt of the earth. That's why I took over this practice, right in the heart of the East End. I was looking forward to hearing more about you from the East Enders who were supposed to rate you high."

'Supposed'.

Rollison's expression did not change.

Marling smacked a clenched fist into the palm of his other hand.

"When I first arrived there wasn't a word raised against you, you were just the hero that my young brother always thought. A few months ago, there was a change in sentiment. You'd left for New York, and rumours started to circulate about Ebbutt, and the way he'd fooled you. You were said to have run away from the Doc, anyhow. It didn't need much to take that a step further—people who'd looked up to you began laughing at you. Ebbutt had taken you in for years, and you didn't know it."

Marling stopped.

Rollison smiled, as if this was the easiest thing to sit and listen to, and he hoped that Marling took due notice as he asked:

"Tell me one thing. How was it you got the ear of the people so quickly?"

"For two reasons," Marling answered promptly. "Just after I came there was a nasty outbreak of typhoid, and with luck and quick work, we got it under control quickly. That broke the ice. The other is that I've always led the conversation round to you when I could. I didn't like what I was hearing—and I still don't like it. Sick people drop their defences much more quickly than most, and—well, I picked up all the gossip I could, simply because I was interested. Now I'm telling you what's being said about Ebbutt. And Ebbutt, apparently, is focussing attention on me."

Rollison nodded.

"If what I hear about him is right, he's probably very edgy just now," Marling said. "It's said that he made hay while you were away, but hoped to get most of his work done before you came back. You returned too soon, and he had to draw you into trouble quickly." Marling sipped the brandy again, and then added with a twisted smile: "So as to get rid of you."

He stopped.

Rollison had waited, until now, to spring his next question: about Esmeralda and this man. Marling looked as if he had recovered from the worst impact of the first shock, and Rollison said:

"How well do you know Esmeralda Gale?"

"Not well enough," Marling said abruptly. "She—she was a friend of my sister. Only a casual friend, I think. Maggie introduced—" he broke off, frowned, and went on abruptly: "It's none of your business."

He closed his eyes, and looked away from the Toff towards the other photograph that was on a small table by his side. It seemed as if talking had taken his mind off the tragedy of his sister; but that the moment he had stopped, his thoughts had flashed to her. It was easy to judge from the tautness of his expression, and from the bleakness of his eyes, just how deeply he was hurt.

Then, he said huskily: "Are you quite sure that the Doc killed her?"

"Yes," said Rollison, and watched the other man narrowly as he went on: "I'm also sure that the Doc has kidnapped Esmeralda Gale."

Marling exclaimed: "Good God! She——" he seemed to catch his breath, and then went on harshly: "Why the hell should he?"

"I don't know. Perhaps to exert pressure, perhaps part of a kind of reign of terror, perhaps because he's some special reason. The fact remains that he kidnapped her."

There was a pause. Then:

"Now *I've* a double personal interest in this business," Marling said roughly. "I tried to keep aloof from it, both sides get sick and I didn't want to keep any patient away. Now, I think it's past time I went to see Ebbutt."

There was murder in his eyes.

"If you see Ebbutt or anyone else until you're back on an even keel, you'll be crazy," Rollison said. "At least wait until to-morrow. If I were you I'd wait until you've heard from me again, I might be able to dig deeper than you."

Marling said, more evenly: "I suppose I'd better not start anything yet, but don't get the idea that this is your job alone."

"Our job," Rollison said, and smiled gently, and stood up. "Mind telling me one other thing?"

"What's that?"

"What made you think I called on you last night?"

Marling's expression eased, and he went to the other side of the desk and picked up a visiting card. It was the familiar faceless man, jaunty and somehow challenging—and one of the cards which Rollison had dropped into the houses the previous night.

"Luke brought this in this morning," he said. "He found a kiddie playing with it in the street. Then he did a bit of snooping, he knows I like the chit-chat, and he came here full of the story. In fact you almost staged a come-back, Rollison—it's the first time anyone has laughed at the Doc since he came on the scene, but there's a lot of tittering this morning. Luke said that he'd heard of eight or nine of these being found, all with people who work for the Doc. You can take it from me that the man in the street would like nothing better than to think you're back in form—*without* Ebbutt."

"Or with Ebbutt cleared?"

Marling said: "That might take a lot more doing than you think, Rollison. There's one thing I haven't told you. The Blue Dog is believed to be the place where many of the messages to the Doc are passed on—through there, and Ebbutt's gymnasium. And there couldn't be a better place."

"No," agreed the Toff, "there couldn't be."

Now he knew exactly what he had to do; and that it must be done at once. He had to force a showdown, and he had to do it alone, or all the respect the East End had for him would be buried in the past.

So might he.

He left Marling five minutes later, feeling quite sure that Marling would return to his study, and pick up that photograph. He did not believe that Marling had lied, and did not think that Marling was the Doc.

But Marling might work for the Doc.

He drove a few hundred yards along the road, and then stopped outside a telephone kiosk. As he went, he was aware of something he hadn't noticed before, but it proved his need to act now. No one nodded, smiled or greeted him in any way, although there were many whom he knew, and who knew him. It was almost as if the people were afraid to admit that they knew the Toff.

He telephoned Grice.

". . . and Bill," he asked, "have you picked up any more information about the woman Jeffson?"

"Yes," Grice answered promptly. "She was the sister of Dr. Marling, a widow who has been living at the Lancing

Hotel for about two years under an assumed name. She had a regular allowance, always paid into her account in cash, and obviously she was the mistress of a pretty wealthy man. We're trying to find out who. That what you want to know?"

"Yes, that's fine," Rollison said. "Any other news in?"

"Nothing at all."

"You haven't picked up Dan Rickett?"

"No, but I'm sure he didn't leave the country," said Grice. "We haven't found his motor-cycle, either."

"Esmeralda?"

"Nothing," Grice said, gruffly, "and that's going to raise the biggest storm yet. Sir John Wylie has a lot of influence in Government circles, and he's beginning to raise Cain. His wife's almost distraught. How well *do* you know the family?"

"No more than I know Esmeralda."

"You can't persuade Wylie to stop throwing his weight about, can you?"

"I can try," said Rollison, cryptically. "Nothing guaranteed."

He rang off, but immediately dialled his own number. Jolly answered almost at once—and something in his man's tone made Rollison pause in what he was going to say.

"What's the excitement, Jolly?"

"If that is the right word, sir," Jolly said. 'There was a note from Miss Gale, sir, which arrived by the last post—she had put her name on the back of the envelope, and I thought I would be wise to open it."

"You were. What does she say?"

"That she thinks she knows who the Doc is," breathed Jolly.

If Esmeralda knew that, no wonder she had been kidnapped.

Would she still be alive?

Rollison told Jolly what he planned to do, rang off, and

went back to the Jaguar. Two small boys were studying it closely, but Rollison was less interested in the children than in three men on the other side of the road, who were standing and watching. They were men who might once have patronized Ebbutt's gymnasium; powerful and tough. They waited until he was at the wheel of the car, and then climbed into their own, and drove after him. He watched them in the driving-mirror; they kept just behind, there was no doubt that they were shadowing him.

The Doc probably wanted a showdown, too.

Rollison turned off the main road, and the other car followed.

There had been a time when to drive through here would be to stage a kind of triumphal procession, but to-day only a few people took the slightest notice of him—and most of those were policemen, who patrolled in pairs. It was a long time since that had been necessary by day.

The other car still followed him.

He turned into the street where the Blue Dog stood at the Mile End Road corner, with the gymnasium just behind it. Half a dozen men lounged about outside the gymnasium, not inside; usually only youngsters who weren't allowed in stayed outside. Rollison pulled up, across the road from the entrance to the big, low-roofed building, and the other car pulled up behind.

He got out.

He was aware of many people watching him from behind their curtains. He caught a glimpse of Liz Ebbutt, at the window of her bedroom. He saw the group of men draw up outside the doorway of the gymnasium. He took out a cigarette as he stepped towards that doorway. The three men followed him, and he knew that they were spreading out, so that he couldn't get away.

The window squealed.

"Mr. Rollison!" Liz Ebbutt screamed at him. "Don't come here, they're waiting for you. Get away!"

He looked up at the window, and grinned and waved. Then he lit the cigarette, and surveyed the five men who were lined up in front of the gymnasium doorway. Inside, he knew, there were several men stripped to the waist, in the middle of training and working out, but stilled, now, with the tension which his coming had brought.

"They'll tear you to bits!" Liz screamed. "Go away, Mr. Rollison, go away!"

This time, Rollison ignored her.

None of the men facing him was familiar, but several of those inside the big shed were cronies of Ebbutt, and once friends of the Toff's. Now, they hung back, as if they were reluctant to show themselves; but none of them made the slightest move to help the Toff.

He put his hand to his pocket.

One of the men said: "Get him," and he heard those behind move towards him, saw those from the doorway crouch, ready to stop him whichever way he tried to go. They were afraid that he had a gun, but all he took from his pocket were his visiting cards. He tossed these into the air so that they billowed out and then began to fall like huge snowflakes—and then he took a running leap towards the doorway. One man dodged. Two drew closer, to stop him. The men from behind were within a yard or two, if they once caught him Liz would be proved right; they would tear him to pieces.

He swerved past the couple, handed another man off, and saw two more blocking the doorway. He had just enough space to take a running leap, and he made for them at speed. As he leapt, they swayed to one side, afraid of being smashed down by his full weight.

He landed just inside the gymnasium, and turned round swiftly; now, his gun was in his hand.

"After all, it's in self defence," he said mildly. "Anyone want to come any further?"

He was not afraid that the men outside would take any chances. His fears were of the men behind, of Ebbutt's men, who should be on his side.

Then, he heard Ebbutt's voice, as the ex-boxer came from the little office in a corner of the shed.

21

SOLO EFFORT

THE Toff stood with his back to Ebbutt and the men inside the gym, and watched the crowd outside. There were nearly a dozen men, now—and, some distance away, many people watching as if they sensed that this was a moment of great decision. The Toff held the automatic lightly in his right hand, watching the Doc's men as they stood still, and then edged away.

"No one coming?" he inquired as if sadly. "That's a pity."

Ebbutt had stopped speaking, and appeared to have stopped moving. No one behind Rollison was nearer than three yards, but that was very near. If they wanted to bring him down, they could do it easily; they could toss Indian clubs at him, or dumb-bells, they could do whatever they liked—*if* they chose to.

Ebbutt would be forced into the open.

A tall, lean-faced man came up the street, hurrying. Someone in the little group outside the gymnasium called:

"Here's Vic!"

Rollison had never heard of Vic. . . .

He didn't like the sneery twist to the man's lips, or the nasty expression in his eyes, or the way his hand was deep in his pocket. He came striding, and the man who had called his name moved towards him.

"What's this all about?" Vic asked, sharply.

"It's the ruddy Torf——"

"I thought I said he wasn't to go inside."

"That's right, that's what you said," the man agreed, "but it's like trying to stop a jet."

Vic sneered: "It's like working with a lot of half-wits."

He kept his right hand in his pocket as he drew nearer the entrance, and as he eyed Rollison, Ebbutt began to speak. Ebbutt's voice was pitched so low that the words only just reached Rollison's ears, and he could imagine that Ebbutt was speaking without moving his lips; so that no one could see that he was talking.

"Mr. Ar," he muttered, "you never should've come, it was askin' fer trouble. Pack it in, woncha? Tell Vic you'll get aht of 'ere quick."

He stopped.

The man named Vic stood two yards from Rollison; if sight of the gun made him uneasy, he didn't show it.

"Just tell 'im you won't make any trouble, Mr. Ar," Ebbutt muttered miserably, "we don't want——"

Vic said flatly:

"Take his gun away, Ebbutt."

Ebbutt drew in a sharp breath.

"You heard me," Vic ordered, "take his gun away, we'll teach him whether he wants to come poking his nose into our front door again. *Take that gun.*"

"Mr. Ar," breathed Ebbutt, "drop the gun, and then make a run for it."

"*Take it!*" rasped Vic.

There was no shadow of doubt what was happening, now. No man behind Rollison would move or speak for him; the friends of yesterday were the neutrals of to-day, and some might even be enemies. There was bitterness in that, but much of it was caused by fear of what reprisals the Doc might take. Ebbutt might be governed by the same fear, but he was coming down on the Doc's side in the showdown.

"Mr. Ar——"

"No, Bill," said Rollison mildly, "I'm not going to drop the gun or give it to you. I've come here because I've a job to do. I want to go down into your cellar."

"Look, that mob out there——"

"I want to have a look round in the cellar," Rollison insisted, "that's what I came for and what I'm going to do."

"Mr. Ar, if you don't drop that gun and talk turkey, there's no knowing wot they'll do. I warned you——"

Rollison spun round.

As he moved, he fired two bullets through the open, sliding door, over the head of Vic and his friends, smacking them into the walls of small houses opposite. Then he drove his right fist into Ebbutt's stomach, and as the big man folded up, staggering and gasping, Rollison jumped towards the sliding door and pulled at it with all his strength, to keep Vic and the others out. He saw Vic dart forward, other men with him. He saw the shiny black cosh in Vic's hand, the ugly weapons in the hands of the others. Vic reached the door and shot out a hand to try to stop it from closing, but Rollison slammed it hard. It crashed into Vic's fingers, and he heard the man's squeal. The door slid back a fraction, Vic's hand dropped out of sight, and Rollison pushed the door right home and dropped the bar across so that it couldn't easily be forced.

Then, he swung round.

A dozen or more men were in here, some with big sweaters, some stripped. Ebbutt was still backing away, but his hands were at his stomach now, and he was breathing heavily.

Heavy thuds shook the sliding door.

"Mind if I look in the cellar, Bill?" Rollison asked politely. He put his gun back into his pocket, as if to suggest that he now knew that he was among friends, and smiled as if there was no hostile crowd outside. He knew that the crowd wouldn't be there long, for the shots would have echoed far and wide—and news of them and news of the assault on the doorway would soon reach the ears of the police. It wouldn't be long before the mob was dispersed, but—it might be too long.

Ebbutt spoke heavily, painfully.

"Mr. Ar, I can't give you no more protection. I told you that, didn't I? I can't take no chances. If I do anyfink to 'elp you, Gawd knows wot'll 'appen to Liz *and* my daughter and '*er* kid."

He stopped, standing squarely in front of Rollison. Men moved behind him, like a solid phalanx, as if to make sure that Rollison couldn't get away. The thudding on the door was thunderous, now. Soon, men would come to the other doorways—those doorways which led to the garden of the Blue Dog, and to the cellar beneath the pub, the cellar where Evie Rickett might have been kept prisoner.

"I just want to go down into the cellar, Bill." Rollison's voice was quite normal. "Give me the keys, will you?"

"Mr. Ar, don't *make* me——"

"Bill," said Rollison lightly, "while I live, nothing and no one is going to stop me from going down into the cellar. Do you want it the hard way?"

" 'Ard way," said Ebbutt, and seemed to sigh. "You're the one wot's makin' it 'ard. Listen to that banging, Mr. Ar, that will tell you 'ow mad they are. You've been away too long, you don't know how——"

There was a splintering noise, behind Rollison; an axe, through the door. Two more thuds followed, and then another menacing crack, as wood splintered. It was only a matter of minutes, now, and the police hadn't arrived; they were probably on the way in force, but they might arrive too late. Ebbutt stood as solid as an oak door, with his men behind him, and others now sidling along the sides.

There was no doubt that Ebbutt was prepared to throw him to the wolves, but—*why*?

The little door in the corner opened, leading to the garden and the cellar.

It might be one of Vic's men, it might be another of Ebbutt's. Rollison didn't know, and didn't care. He moved very swiftly, taking the gun from his pocket. That made the men behind Ebbutt sway back, as if before a high wind; but Ebbutt stood his ground.

"Bill," said Rollison, "I'm coming."

"For Gawd's sake——" Ebbutt was sweating, there was a beading on his forehead and face, a beading on his upper lip. "Don't make it any worse, Mr. Ar, if you get down into that cellar my Liz an' Maisie an' ner kid——"

Rollison squeezed the trigger.

He fired at Ebbutt's fleshy thigh, but aimed to frighten, not to wound. The roar of the shot sounded loud in the confined space, and the corrugated iron clanged under the explosive sound; and under the smashing blows of the axe. Then Rollison thrust Ebbutt aside, and he staggered back, the sweat dripping from his forehead, one hand clutching his leg. The other men, nervous of the gun, moved away—but before Rollison was half-way along the gymnasium, a man picked up an Indian club and flung it at him. It passed in front of his eyes. Another caught him on the back, a third brushed the side of his head. But the threat of the gun cleared a path ahead, and he was within a yard of the door when he saw who had opened it.

It was Liz Ebbutt, in her Salvation Army uniform.

She stood just outside the door, and something shimmered in her hand. A knife? *Liz?* Rollison couldn't believe it. A dumb-bell struck him a glancing blow on the back of the head, and it wouldn't be long before the other door crashed in. If Vic and the mob caught up with him, he would probably be beaten to death before the police arrived.

But he couldn't strike *Liz*.

He saw her lips move, and saw her hold out the 'thing' which shimmered in her hand.

"That's the cellar key," she said, in a quavering voice, "as God's my judge I don't know what's down there, but there's the key. Hurry, Mr. Rollison, or else——"

The door behind them gave way. Rollison heard it crash, then glanced over his shoulder and saw Vic and the others spilling towards him. The ring was in their way, and he had only seconds to spare. He moved swiftly outside and as he did so Liz Ebbutt slammed and locked the small door, and said:

"Hurry, won't you? Please *hurry*."

There were the big wooden gates which led from the

back of the Blue Dog to the street—and the gates were being forced open, as men pushed against them. Two men were looking over the wall from the far side, but it wasn't easy to climb, because Ebbutt had covered it with barbed wire and broken glass. There was the back of the pub, and the steps leading down to the cellar—and the cellar door.

"*There he is!*" a man roared.

Now, they were beating on the back door of the gymnasium. The noise was deafening, and it drowned other sounds, for the corrugated iron walls boomed and clanged as the door shook. Rollison reached the cellar steps and started down them. A man atop the wall flung something at him; iron clanged as it hit the ground. He had to turn his back, and bend down, to thrust the key into the lock. If he'd had to pick the lock, he wouldn't have had a chance.

He felt the key turn, and thrust the door open.

It was dark inside, and the smell of beer was almost overpowering. He didn't wait, but jumped in and slammed the door behind him. He locked it, then took out his hooded torch and flashed the narrow beam of light round.

He found the main lights, and switched them on. He heard the sounds, muted now, and fancied that he heard a footstep in the yard. He pushed home the top and bottom bolts of the heavy door, and then turned to look about the cellar. Here, barrels of beer stood on trestles round the walls, each with a wooden bowl beneath it, to catch drops as they dripped. Smaller barrels were on shelves, above the big ones below. At the other side of the cellar was another door, and he knew that this led to the wine bins and the spirit bins and the bottle store. He might need another key for that. He reached the door, hearing the distant sounds but no battering on this one.

Yet.

He twisted the handle, and pushed and pulled, but the door wouldn't open. He tried the key, but it was too big. He was clenching his teeth as he took out a penknife with a picklock blade, and started to work on the lock. He felt it catch, and then slip. He wasn't as steady as he should be and fought hard for self-control. In the back of his mind was a fear which had been there from the beginning—that he would find Esmeralda, with the evidence that Ebbutt was involved.

There was another fear, in its way greater.

That the Doc's men would throw an 'egg'; as they had threatened at his flat, as they had done at the hotel.

The key gripped.

He turned it slowly and cautiously. Sweat was running down his cheeks and forehead. He felt the lock turning, but if it slipped again he would have to start afresh, and he might not have time. He felt it slip back sharply, and knew that he had won this battle against time, but as he pushed at the door, there was a heavy thudding on the other door which led from the garden.

Here they came again.

Torch flashing, he went into the darker cellars beyond this one. He stabbed at the light switch, and lights blazed on as he slammed the door behind him. He shot these bolts, too, then leaned against the door, as if he had to pause to get his breath back.

There were the long lines of bins, the bottles covered with dust and cobwebs, the whisky and gin and vermouths, the rums and the smaller bottles fairly clean. He saw no one and nothing else, but that wasn't significant; this part of the cellar was like a rabbit warren, with passages leading off to the right and left. Until he had searched them all, he couldn't be sure what was here. The bins themselves were open at the sides, here and there bottles had toppled from one bin into another.

He stopped, abruptly.

An empty bin was close to the spot where two passages intersected. In this was piled a collection that would not have shamed the Black Museum at Scotland Yard. There were knives and guns, coshes and pieces of lead piping, there was a hangman's rope, coiled in and out of the other oddments, there were little phials of poison, there was even a broken cuckoo clock and a brim of a top hat, poking out of the heap.

Here were his trophies, part of the thing he had come to find.

He did not see the laddered nylon stocking, which had been worn by Jessica Gay, who had sacrificed herself for love of the Doc.

22

THE 'EGG'

THE thudding on the door sounded further away, but the reverberation made bottles bang slightly against each other, and there was a continual rattling sound. Little pieces of straw fluttered from the bins. There was no other sound, and no threat from the other end of the cellar—with stairs leading from the pub itself. Rollison began to move very fast, trying not to think of all the implications of what he had seen, desperately anxious for Esmeralda, desperately fearful of the possibility of fire.

Then, he saw the girl.

She was lying in another empty bin—actually across two of them. Her head was propped up at an awkward angle against bottles of whisky, and her knees were bent. She didn't seem to be breathing. Rollison reached her, and for a moment was oblivious of everything else. He bent over her, the smell of whisky and of straw strong in his nostrils, and took her hand, feeling for the pulse.

It was beating.

He could see no signs of external injury, and he didn't lose much time, but eased her forward out of the bins, then lifted her. Her head lolled forward helplessly; obviously she was drugged.

Now, he heard the banging again.

If he went up the stairs leading into the Blue Dog itself, what chance would he have?

He put Esmeralda carefully down on a barrel which was upturned at the foot of the stairs, leaned her against a post by the stairs, and went up, pressing against the hatch cover with his hands. He couldn't move it. The bolts on the outside would be shot, so he couldn't get out that way. He stopped wasting his breath and his energy, and turned back to Esmeralda. In her unconsciousness, she looked fresh and charming; and there could be no gleam in her eyes to suggest that she was intent on fooling him.

Never mind how she looked!

He could wait here and hope for rescue by the police—but the police might be too late. The most likely danger was an attack with one of the eggs, and if the cellar was fired, from the garden end, he would have no chance at all. It would be all over in a few minutes. The wooden barrels, the spirits, the straw, the shelving, would catch alight, the fire would roar through the cellars, devouring everything.

He couldn't get out through the pub.

He picked Esmeralda up and carried her towards the other end, and had to pass his forlorn-looking trophies. He still heard the hammering on this inside door, which must be more solid than the other.

There were the trophies——

He stopped short, with Esmeralda cradled in his arms, and he stared at the bin next to the trophies. When he had passed it from the other direction, he had thought that it was empty, but it wasn't. It looked like a nest in which a chicken had laid large eggs so addled that the shells were discoloured. There were four 'eggs' in all, and they were close together on the straw, looking unbelievably innocent. But for the one which had been set at the top of the door at his flat, he would not have given these a second thought, but here were *the* 'eggs'.

He put Esmeralda down, slowly.

There were heavier noises from the door.

He picked up one of the eggs, very carefully, then selected a handful of straw from another bin, put this in his left hand, and put the 'egg' on that; it was steadier. He glanced at the girl and her pale beauty, then walked steadily towards the door. He wasn't surprised to see light through it; they hadn't been able to force it down, and they were splintering it as they had the gymnasium door.

He saw the blade of the axe.

It was wrenched out, and he could imagine the man wielding it drawing back and pausing for breath; there was a moment of quiet. He fancied that he could hear heavy breathing, and he wondered how many men were waiting to rush inside.

He called, clearly: "That you, Vic?"

He heard a man gasp.

"Don't be shy," he urged, "if you're Vic, admit it."

"What——" a man began.

"Listen, Rollison," broke in the man named Vic. His voice had the unmistakable edge of cruelty. "Nothing can help you now, don't get any ideas. Before the police can get here you'll be just a heap of blood and bones. After this——"

"No armistice terms?" asked Rollison, sweetly.

There was a pause.

"You won't get any terms," Vic said at last, "you won't even get a decent burial, there won't be enough of you left." He paused again—and soon there came a crashing blow from the axe. Rollison caught sight of the blade shimmering in the electric light. As the wielder tugged to get it out, Vic went on raspingly:

"Your friends the police can't get into the street, we've got cars across it each end—the riot outside that will last for hours. You wanted a showdown now, you've got it. The Doc won't need *any* more building up, after this. He'll have the police so scared——"

Crash, fell the axe.

"That they'll come round here in parties of a dozen, not in pairs," Vic gibed, "and they won't have that ruddy stool pigeon called the Toff——"

Crash.

Now, the wood split wide open, and for a moment Rollison caught a glimpse of the shaft of the axe and also of Vic's face; then the blade was withdrawn, and the wood came together again, but it wouldn't take long to get the door down now; it was all over bar the shouting.

If the street was barricaded——

It was.

Superintendent Grice jumped out of the police car at about the time that Rollison saw the wood of the door split asunder. He could not get nearer than a hundred yards to the Blue Dog, because of the huge crowd. Police were trying to force a line of traffic through, but the crowd was almost out of hand. Over the heads of the people, Grice saw the cars which were drawn across the road near the Blue Dog, their wheels sticking up in the air; they had been turned upside down, so that they couldn't be easily pushed away.

He saw bottles flying through the air, and could smell the foul fumes of stink-bombs which kept smacking against the pavement, the roadway and the walls of houses. There was a powerful smell of ammonia, too. Now and again a section of the crowd stampeded, to get out of the way of flying glass or liquid, but most of the crowd was safely out of range. About forty policemen were in the line of fire, and two men were sitting against the wall of a small house, blood streaming down their faces. The windows and the doorways of the Blue Dog were barricaded, and at the top windows men stood hurling missiles at the police, who couldn't get near.

With three policemen to clear a path for him, Grice got as near the end of the street as he could. A Divisional Superintendent came up, grimly.

"Hallo, Bill, glad you're here to see it with your own

eyes. After this, perhaps you'll wish you'd stopped your pal Rollison from throwing his weight about."

"Where is he?"

"The last anyone saw of him, he was going into the gymnasium. There's a rumour that he's in the cellar. All I can tell you is that he fired a couple of shots, probably to make sure we came quick. I sent a couple of cars at the double, but they were overturned as soon as they stopped, the chaps in them were badly beaten up. The Doc's in earnest."

Grice said: "When wasn't he?" He began to move nearer to the line of overturned cars. A bottle smashed close to his feet, and liquid sprayed from it; he caught his breath as the ammonia bit at him.

The Divisional man coughed and moved hastily away.

"Just went mad," he said hoarsely. "As soon as I heard what was happening I called you, but before we could get enough men here, they'd gone stark raving mad. Know what this is, don't you?"

"The Doc would like it to be a final showdown."

"If you ask me he's got a chance to win," the Divisional man said, almost desperately. "We'll pick up a few of his legmen when this is over, but I don't think we'll get to him—not with any proof of identity anyhow. And if we can't bring him in, then he'll be cock of the walk for a hell of a long time. Rollison as the Toff will just be forgotten."

Grice said slowly: "He's pretty tough."

"They're after his blood, and they're going to get it," the Divisional man said, "he won't ever come out of this lot alive."

Grice didn't speak.

Then he saw Jolly, much nearer the barricade than any other civilian, talking to a C.I.D. man. Jolly's face was as white as his shirt, and there was a scared look in his eyes as he stared at the Blue Dog and then, espying Grice, came slowly towards him.

Grice knew that Jolly also feared that there was no chance.

• • • •

Rollison waited until the axe blade smacked into the door again. This time the noise was not so loud, and wood splintered loosely. Half a dozen more blows and it would all be over—if Vic had his way. The man's lean face, with those twisted, thin lips, showed for a moment, and then vanished as the wood closed up.

"Vic, you couldn't be making a mistake, could you?" Rollison inquired clearly. "I've found the eggs, you see. In fact, I have one in my hand at the moment. Addled, but no doubt capable of bursting. It would probably make quite a noise."

Another smashing blow from the axe was due.

It didn't come.

"A little thing and a pretty little thing, although I confess I may be prejudiced in its favour this time," said Rollison blithely. "It would be a pity if I dropped it, wouldn't it? Of course, I would roast, but so would you. And the others with you, too. How does the prospect appeal?"

A man said, hoarsely: "Think he's got one?"

Vic didn't answer.

"Oh, I have one," Rollison assured the speaker briskly, "It's the largest of the four which had been laid in the bin near my trophies of the chase. What shall I use as a souvenir this time, Vic? Eggshell? It will have to be a substitute, I wouldn't like to use any of the real thing. Shall I open the door?" He paused for a moment, and then added: "Remember, if I were to be shot or knocked down or otherwise shaken, the egg would fall and that would be very much that, wouldn't it? Forgive me if I sound a little light-headed, it's simply that I'm really light-hearted for the first time to-day."

He moved cautiously, and pushed back one bolt; pushed back another. He could see through a hole in the door that the other men were still there, but a little further away, and he believed that they were waiting to see the 'egg' with their own eyes. He pulled open the door, slowly, and thrust his hand through—so that they could see that he was telling the simple truth.

"To coin a phrase," he said, "its mother was some chicken. Who was its mother, Vic? Or did it only have a doc?"

The door opened wide.

Vic and half a dozen other men were in the outer cellar, among the big beer barrels, moving slowly away from him. The far door was open, and Rollison could see the steps and the feet of other men atop them. One of the men here started to back up the stairs.

"I shouldn't," chided Rollison, "it isn't fair on your pals. I mean, if any of you are to be burned to ashes, fair play suggests that all should be." The man stopped dead, and Rollison smiled at him amiably. "Supposing you do a little job for me. Come back here, go inside and pick up Esmeralda Gale, and then carry her after me. Be careful you don't knock against me," he added solemnly, "we wouldn't like that, would we, Vic?"

Vic licked his lips.

The other man came forward, slowly.

"By the way, and as a point of interest, who is the Doc?" Rollison asked, as if he was only casually interested. "I have formed my own conclusion, of course, but I'd like to hear it in the form of a statement from one of his men."

Vic muttered: "You—you know who he is."

"Yes, but do you?"

"No," Vic said, "I don't know him from Adam."

He broke off, as if he was choking.

The other man came just behind Rollison, carrying Esmeralda.

"On second thoughts, you'd better get in front of me," said Rollison, "then I can see what you're doing. Gangway, please. *Here, mind my egg!*" He started, as if the man had jogged his hand, and there was a frightened gasp from nearly every man there. He covered the 'egg' gently with his free hand, and shook his head at it. "We don't want you hatching yet," he upbraided. "Forward, please, and give me plenty of elbow room."

The man carrying Esmeralda went forward, up the steps,

into the yard. There was another crowd; still and silent here, although there was plenty of noise from the street. Bill Ebbutt and Liz were near the gymnasium door, Ebbutt dwarfing his wife, and standing still as death.

"Pass the word along that I'm coming with enough high explosive to blow everyone here to their Maker," said Rollison. "Ah, Doctor Ebbutt, I presume, and Doc for short. Not badly hurt, I see. Be kind enough to take Miss Gale from this knight errant, and carry her out yourself, that will be a fitting climax." He didn't look at Liz; and Liz was leaning backwards, her hands at her face, as if she could not find the courage to look at any of them. Not even her Army uniform sustained her.

"Mr. Ar——" Ebbutt said, and gulped, and then tried again: "Mr. Ar, I—I noo they was using the cellar, they—they pinched my gran'child. I—I 'ad to do what they said. They made me give them a set o' keys, but I didn't know——"

"Oh, Doctor," said Rollison reproachfully, "must we add lies to our ugly past? Take Esmeralda." He waited until Ebbutt had taken the girl, handling her with surprising gentleness, and then he said: "Onward, please." He drew level with Liz, and he put his arm round her shoulders—and the crowd gasped because the 'egg' quivered. "Come on, Liz," Rollison encouraged, "remember the old saw, it's always darkest before dawn."

"As God is my judge," Liz Ebbutt said, "I didn't know."

"Of course you didn't know," Rollison said. "But stand close, you'll be all right now. Hey, Charlie," he added to one of Ebbutt's oldest cronies, "tell the boys to take the glad tidings outside, I've the most powerful egg in the universe raring to hatch."

The man gulped. "Sure, okay." He grabbed two others. "Come on, you 'eard 'im." They went across the gymnasium, and the people in there crouched away from Rollison, from Liz, and from Ebbutt and the girl. The little procession reached the battered door, and the bright daylight of the street. Ebbutt's cronies went ahead, and the

Doc's men, crouching behind the barricade with their bottles of ammonia, their stink-bombs and everything they could use as missiles, heard what was said and looked round and drew fearfully back from the Toff.

"Now pull one of the cars away," Rollison ordered.

Men hurried to obey.

The crowd was silenced everywhere. No missiles were thrown. The only sound was the scraping of the roof of the car on the road, and the heavy breathing of the men who heaved at it. Soon there was a wide enough gap for Ebbutt and his wife to get through. Beyond this, Rollison saw Grice—and also saw Jolly, who looked as radiant as a child at Christmas. He had his hands clasped together, as if in thanksgiving.

Grice came hurrying.

"Take it easy, Bill," Rollison urged. "I know you won't believe any of it, but this little thing in my hand could cause a long queue at the funeral parlours. You might fix a few things for me, by the way—downstairs in the cellar there are all the pretty-pretties which used to be on my wall. I'd like them salvaged. There are probably some other little souvenirs as well—three more of these."

Grice looked at the 'egg'.

"Be careful with that," he said, in a voice which sounded weak from this new shock. "I'll get a container for it." He gave a sergeant instructions, then looked away from Rollison towards Ebbutt and the pale figure of his wife, and he went on in a harder voice: "William Ebbutt, it is my duty to arrest you on a charge of inciting to violence, and I have to warn you that anything you say may be used in evidence." He broke off, and moistened his lips, then turned to the Divisional man, who was just coming up. "Take the girl, will you, and then use the handcuffs on Eb——"

"Not yet," pleaded the Toff, "be gentle, William." He gave first Grice and then Ebbutt a curious look, but Ebbutt did not notice it, and Grice seemed startled. "Ebbutt isn't the Doc, you know," the Toff went on. "He didn't work for the Doc until a short while ago, when his grand-daughter was kidnapped, and he was told that unless he did what he was told, she would never be seen alive again. Isn't that so, Bill?"

Ebbutt, who was easing Esmeralda into a policeman's arms, swung round towards the Toff, with his eyes blazing with new hope. The constable took the girl. Two plain-clothes men moved forward quickly, one of them flashing handcuffs. Liz still by her husband's side, raised her hands towards the Toff in a kind of supplication.

"Now, look, Rolly——" protested Grice.

"Facts are facts and facts are stubborn things," said Rollison prosily, "and I don't mind admitting I could do with a drink and a cigarette. Take this damned thing away, will you?" He waited until one of the detectives came forward, carrying a box lined with yellow dusters, and took the 'egg' with great care. "Thanks. And don't drop it," Rollison added warningly, "it might break. Where was I? Oh, yes—this fabulous, fabled Doc. Not Bill Ebbutt. After all, Esmeralda Gale didn't know our Bill, did she Bill? So when she wrote and told Jolly that she thought she could name the Doc, she didn't mean him. I'd like to know how she found out, but I'm quite sure she found the right man."

Grice said abruptly: "Well, who?"

23

ESMERALDA'S CLUE

GRICE's 'well, who?' seemed to echo up and down the street, to be thrown back from the upturned cars and from the tense faces of the men and women in the crowd. Grice was no less on edge than any of them. Rollison didn't answer at once, but looked at Esmeralda's fair, curly hair—and then saw Dr. Jonathan Marling come from the edge of the crowd, allowed to pass by the police. He walked with long strides in a steady, confident manner. Grice saw the way Rollison looked at him, and motioned to two sergeants. They moved so that they could stand on either side of Marling when he drew level.

"You sure?" asked Grice, *sotto voce*.

"I'm sure that Esmeralda wants a doctor," Rollison said, and saw the anxiety on Marling's face fade as he drew level. "They aren't strangers, either." Marling heard that, glanced at him sharply, but didn't speak until he was by Esmeralda's side. Then he said in a taut voice:

"Let me look at her."

"Dr. Marling——" Grice began.

"Sorry if I misled you, Bill," said Rollison, "I didn't imply that I thought Marling is *the* Doc—in fact I agreed about the thing which made that almost certainly untrue from the beginning." He watched as Marling felt for Esmeralda's pulse and then lifted her eyelids, very gently. "If a real doctor was the Doc, then Doc was the one soubriquet he wouldn't use. Don't you think so?"

Grice said: "Rolly, I know you've had a rough time and we're grateful for what you've done, but don't keep talking for the sake of it. If you know who the Doc is, say so. If you don't——" his gaze shifted sharply, to the agonized Ebbutt.

"I think I know," Rollison said, drawing at the cigarette; and then someone came forward with a whisky flask, and he unscrewed the cap and took a swallow, gratefully. "Ah, wonderful. Scotland for aye. No, don't take it away—I'll want another in a minute! Where was I?" He looked at Grice, who had almost unending patience, and then he went on:

"The first thing is really cheating. You weren't present when Sir John Wylie saw Jessica Gay's stocking on my trophy wall. A man can hide a great deal, but Wylie couldn't hide the momentary glimpse of sheer hatred when he saw the stocking there. I didn't let him see that I'd noticed, but from then on I began to wonder why he'd forced himself and his party on to me that evening. At first I'd blamed it on to Esmeralda, but looking back I could see that Wylie was really responsible. I'm pretty sure, now, that he'd heard a rumour that Rickett was coming to me for help, and hoped to find out all about it, posing as a kind of interested spectator. He'd threatened the Rickett baby, of course, and when he heard the child at the flat, he wouldn't take long to guess whose it was.

"When he virtually suggested that his wife should take care of the infant, I agreed because I felt sure that it wouldn't come to any harm while it was at the house, and I thought the necessary precautions were taken against it disappearing. I'd misjudged his ingenuity, and the courage of some of the men who worked for him.

"Once the child was kidnapped, I had just one thing to do—get it back unharmed. I owed that child life.

"Still, I was after proof of Wylie's guilt, and it took some finding, but when Esmeralda wrote and said she thought she knew the Doc, and when she disappeared—well, that seemed a straight pointer to Wylie, too."

Grice said harshly: "But the *proof*, Rolly?"

Rollison looked at Esmeralda, who was still unconscious. "There," he said.

She came round, soon afterwards, and when she was able to talk she said almost in a crying voice:

"Did you know—my uncle is the Doc?"

"It was pointing his way," Rollison, "but what makes you so sure?"

"I went to say good-bye to him before I left his house," said Esmeralda. "Jane was out, he was in his dressing-room. There was a crumpled nylon stocking on the dressing-table, I suppose he thought I'd believe it was Jane's, but——"

"It was Jessica Gay's," said Rollison.

"Yes, I knew it at once," Esmeralda said, "there was a touch of scarlet nail varnish, for a run, and Jane only uses natural. I tried to pretend not to notice but could see that he knew I had. I expected him to try to scare me into saying nothing, or even to run away, but I didn't dream of what he would do."

Grice turned and gave orders to men from the Yard, while ambulance men looked after Esmeralda.

Rollison stopped again, and this time he didn't have any of the whisky, but he lit another cigarette. The police were getting control of the crowd, and other police were removing the barriers, after a chain of arrests which would keep the magistrates very busy next morning, and the prison gates swinging briskly. Grice and the other C.I.D. men seemed prepared to wait for Rollison to go on.

Instead, Ebbutt said: "I swear I never did a fing for 'im until Maisie's kid was snatched, and then he told me he was going to use me cellar. I just 'adn't the guts to say no, Mr. Ar. I didn't tell no one, not even Liz."

"It comes to something when a man can't confide in the woman who's been his lawful wedded spouse for twenty-nine years," barked Liz Ebbutt. "Don't be such a fool again."

"He won't," said Rollison, and added curiously: "Bill, is it true you spend a fortune in pensioning off has-beens?"

"I don't spend any more than you do, Mr. Ar," said Ebbutt flatly. "I make a profit aht of the gym and promoting a few fights, and the pub looks arter me and Liz. We've got enough, so we gives the rest away."

"I want to make sure that Grice knows that," said Rollison.

Marling joined the group near him, and the Ebbutts drew away. There was unstinting admiration in Marling's eyes when he spoke.

"Now I really have a story for my young brother," he said. "I hope they give you the George Medal. I even forgive you for not waiting for me, too. That couldn't have been because you didn't trust me, could it?"

"Couldn't it?" asked Rollison, lightly. "You, or your odd job man, Luke—I thought it much more likely that Luke was the Doc's man, that your surgery was used for taking messages and serving as a kind of clearing house, when you weren't there. But whether I suspected you or not, this was a job I had to do on my own."

"Or for ever hide your head in shame," agreed Marling. "You'll rise as high as a shooting star after this. Mind telling me if Ebbutt was the only one who seemed to point a finger at me?"

"Oh, no," said Rollison. "Esmeralda did. She had your photograph and you had hers." He grinned as he realized what an admission he had made when he revealed his knowledge of that. "Early on, remember, Esmeralda might have told the Doc where to find the baby. Your sister pointed to you, too, as your photograph was in her apartment, and hers was here."

Marling's smile faded.

"I see," he said.

"Doc Marling," said Rollison gently, "you shouldn't take that too hard. You hadn't seen much of Maggie for a long time. Being your twin, it hurt the more, but—if she'd lived she would be in a lot of trouble now, and you wouldn't enjoy what you'd have to hear about her. Now the police and the newspapers will be much more interested in the living than the dead."

"I suppose you're right," Marling conceded, slowly. "Thanks, Toff."

Then, Jolly, who had been hovering, came up and made himself felt, insisting that it was past time that Mr. Rollison had a meal. It did not greatly matter where, but——

Ebbutt said huskily: "Mr. Ar, you wouldn't like to come an' 'ave a bite wiv us, would you?"

"Can Jolly come too?" asked the Toff, and then to Grice: "See if you can make one of them tell you where Rickett is, Bill."

Rickett was found in a small room at the gymnasium, his nose broken, his body black and blue from 'persuasion'. He had not told Vic or any of the Doc's men where he had hidden the big haul, but when he saw Rollison and heard what had happened, he said thickly.

"I'll make a statement, Mr. Rollison, and get it over. You'll try to make it easy for me, won't you?"

"Yes. So will the police," Rollison assured him.

"That's maybe," Rickett said, and went on abruptly: "Sure Evie's okay?"

"She's like the baby. Fine."

Rickett screwed his bruised face into a smile.

Then a messenger came hurrying.

"Mr. Grice would like a word with you on the radio telephone, sir."

"Thanks," said Rollison, and hurried to a police car. As he drew within sight of the crowd which was several thousands strong, there was a burst of cheering. For years, nothing had done him so much good as that.

He waved, and ducked into the car.

"In trouble, Bill?" he asked, mildly.

That surprised Grice into a chuckle.

"Not so deeply as some people," he said. "Rolly, we've got Wylie. He tried to bluff it out, but the nylon stocking beat him—he still had it in a suit in his wardrobe. Not much doubt he was desperately in love with Jessica Gay, and—but I can give you details later. I——"

"Anything else on Wylie?"

"Oh, yes, plenty. Lists of names and addresses including your man Vic, Jessica Gay, Maggie Jeffson and others we picked up this afternoon."

"His wife?" Rollison asked, quietly.

"I don't think she was really surprised," Grice said. "And I think we'll find that Jessica Gay wasn't his first and Maggie Jeffson wasn't his last mistress. Lady Wylie knew he wasn't exactly a faithful husband. From what we've pieced together so far, he went into it years ago, looking for easy money, and began to see himself as an underworld king. The old, old story, lust for power."

"Yes," Rollison said, "I see."

"I can tell you why he wanted your trophies," Grice went on. "You'd taken them as souvenirs of cases which ended like the case of Jessica Gay. He wanted Jessica's stocking, but he didn't want to take that alone. Take one, take all. He was going to make a public bonfire of them, and make a fool of you."

"He probably doesn't know how close he was," Rollison said. "Thanks again, Bill."

He left the police car, and another cheer was raised, but he felt subdued in spirit, and was cheered up only by sight of Esmeralda, looking almost herself again, and leaning on Marling's arm.

Rollison told her what he had heard from Grice.

"I must go to Jane, quickly," Esmeralda said. "Darling, is your car——"

"Before you go," said Rollison quietly, "tell me why you first called on Jonathan Marling. Not the charity appeal excuse—the real reason."

Esmeralda did not hesitate.

"It's really very simple," she said. "I knew that my uncle often had *affaires*, and I saw him in a restaurant with a very lovely woman—this Maggie. It wasn't very hard to scrape an acquaintance with her. I was going to plead with her to give uncle up, but—well, I didn't get round to it. For one thing, she was so nice, and Aunt—well, anyway, I didn't. One day, she introduced me to her brother, and somehow he was the only one of the family who mattered from then on."

Marling's fingers were very tight about her arm; and they looked at each other as if there was no one else in the world. But Marling said:

"Please God it always stays that way, but—now we've got to go to your Aunt Jane."

There wasn't much else, Rollison reflected, a day or two

later. The story was already fading from the headlines, but no one was ever likely to know all the details. Perhaps they didn't matter. There were the good things. Dan Rickett, was likely to get a short sentence for his theft, for he had returned everything he had stolen; he would keep as straight as his Evie could keep him, when he came out.

There was Esmeralda and her doctor.

It was known, now, that Marling's surgery was used a great deal for the other Doc's men to meet, exchange messages and pass on orders—that was why they had all been on Marling's roll of patients. Luke had been in charge of this, completely unsuspected by Marling.

When Rollison reached Gresham Terrace, much later, it was dusk, and street lights were already on. He went quietly up to his flat, and as he reached the door, Jolly opened it.

"So you still have eyes at the back of your head," said Rollison, mildly. "Always keep them open, they can come in useful."

"I'll certainly try, sir," said Jolly, and he followed Rollison into the study-cum-living-room.

Rollison stopped abruptly, and surveyed the trophy wall. Jolly had arranged another miracle, for the whole wall had been re-papered; he had been busy, too, fitting brackets and generally preparing for the ceremony of replacing the trophies.

"I trust you approve of the plain cream background, sir, I thought that the exhibits themselves would add all the colour that is required," he said. "Ebbutt telephoned early this morning, and I took the liberty of saying that he and Mrs. Ebbutt will be welcome this evening, sir—subject to postponement if you should have any other engagement, of course—and I understand that they are to bring everything that was taken away from here. Nothing was seriously damaged."

"That's fine," said Rollison. "In fact, that's wonderful. What—er—trophy do you suggest for this case, Jolly?"

"If you will allow," said Jolly, "I would mount and

frame a photograph of the Rickett infant. Tinted, perhaps, and quite small. Will that serve, sir?"

"Perfectly," said Rollison, "provided it's taken in the nude, and you take the photograph."

THE END